LIBBY'S CHALLENGE

A HERITAGE RECLAIMED

BY

BILL SANDS

Bill Mason

ISBN: 1-4392-6109-1
ISBN-13: 9781439261095

Visit www.booksurge.com to order additional copies.

Front cover photo by the author; Trapper Creek Lodge, Darby, Montana 59829.

This physical location was the inspiration for the following fictitious story.

DISCLAIMER

The story contained within this book is fictional and in no way represents actual characters or events. All of these activities and individuals are figments of the author's imagination, and any similarities to actual happenings, or to real persons living or dead, is purely coincidental.

OTHER TITLES BY BILL SANDS

Big Sky and Beyond
Short story collection
Montana Related, Backwoods

Off Soundings
Short story collection
Ocean Related, Boating, Ships

What Awaits the Dawn
Short story collection
Montana Related

They Who Dared
Short story collection
Montana Related and Yachting

Donavan Creek
Modern Western

Alone / Together
Science Fiction

I Will Not Die
Short story collection
Montana Related

BILL SANDS

Bill Sands lives on the North Olympic Peninsula of Washington State far removed from his birthplace and childhood in Massachusetts. He spent a period of his early adulthood living in Tennessee before moving to Montana. He is a veteran of both the U.S. Navy, and the Army National Guard, logging a combined total of over seventeen years in the two services. He is married with four children and a host of other descendants. He has lived in the contemporary settings of small towns as well as wilderness locations in the Montana wilds. For a period of years he operated a small cattle ranch in Montana and then followed other family members moving westward to Washington State. Here he was involved in a commercial fishing enterprise captaining his own salmon troller and longline boat. In his retirement years he has furthered his boating interests spending long summers in remote British Columbia waters enjoying his leisure time with his wife and faithful dog Edward.

CONTENTS

CHAPTER I
The Festive Season
December 18–25, 1998

"Good morning America! Here we are in the home of our struggling '76ers. Obviously they miss Julius Irving's contribution. But more on that later... Right now? Let's see, it's 7:30 in the morning on a crisp and windy Friday, the eighteenth of December, 1998. Let's get with it everyone, there's only five more shopping days till Christmas. Hey, Mom! Better hurry up and get those young students off to school... Now for the latest on our local scene and some highlights around the Keystone state... Last night firefighters were called..."

Libby Emerson reached up and switched off the small radio mounted beneath her kitchen cabinet next to the range. She turned back the sleeves of her housecoat and began washing the breakfast dishes. Her husband, Bill, had left for work some time ago, and through the kitchen window she watched as her ten-year-old son, Michael, ran with his little dog down the long landscaped driveway toward the road. Three other children waited there. Mike's timing had been perfect. Just as he arrived the school bus wheeled into sight with its warning lights flashing. The door swung open, and the small group of children climbed aboard. Mike's sheltie, Skipper, sat quietly for a moment sadly watching as the bus pulled away, and then he dashed back toward the house as was his custom. Except for Skipper, Libby was now alone.

The dishwashing chores were soon completed, the dishes put away, and Libby poured herself another cup of strong black coffee. She sat quietly at the kitchen table enjoying the peace and quiet and studied the daily paper's crossword puzzle for long minutes. She finally rose, located a pencil on the small desk by the back door, and returned to the table. She worked on the impossible puzzle for some time and then in disgust tossed the paper into the recycle tub beneath her sink.

Libby toured her roomy colonial-style house as she set her priorities for the day. Mike had made his bed in an acceptable fashion, and it stood in stark opposition to what Libby found as she glanced into her own spacious bedroom. In the bathroom she spent several minutes combing and brushing her long brunette hair fashioning it into a sweeping ponytail. She dabbed a touch of neutral shade lipstick on her full lips and hung her housecoat on the back of the bathroom door. She made her big queen-size bed in jig time, after which she finished dressing by slipping into a comfortable pair of jeans and a blouse. From the closet she retrieved a bag of gifts that needed to be wrapped before the coming holiday.

She paused in the living room and adjusted several bright ornaments hanging on her Christmas tree. She was always proud of her tree, and this year was no exception. The decorating had taken over three hours using both Mike and Bill's help to complete the project. It had been a happy and joyous occasion for them all. The traditional event, with the house full of Christmas carols and holiday incense spurred their good spirits of festive cheer to a new level of anticipation. Libby smiled as she recalled the event. Several minutes later she was busy wrapping gifts on her kitchen table. The phone rang, and with a puzzled grunt of surprise, she lifted the receiver.

Libby frowned. "Morning," she greeted cheerfully.

"Morning yourself," came the surprising voice of her husband.

"Traffic bad today?"

"Not too bad, but the bus was packed. Made it into the city in better than the usual time. You have any plans for tonight?"

Libby thought for a moment. "No, nothing special. Why?"

"You don't remember?"

"Remember what?" Libby asked, puzzled.

"What's today's date?"

Libby rolled her wrist over and glanced at her watch. "Friday, the eighteenth…" She paused for a long moment. "Oh my God, Bill. I'm sorry… Happy anniversary."

"Just dawned on me too, on the way into the city. We're going out on the town tonight. You deserve it after putting up with me for ten years. Get us a babysitter for the evening. I'll take her back home when we get in."

"No big party, Bill. Just the two of us, OK?"

"Suits me."

"Nothing formal either."

"Wear your jeans if you'd like. We'll go roller-skating after we eat."

"Sounds great. See you when, about six o'clock as usual?"

"Yes. See you then… Love you!"

"Love you too."

Libby's audible kiss completed their call. She located her address book and a moment later was in contact with their usual babysitter's mother. She ended the call a minute later with a frown of worry spreading across her face. She thumbed through the pages of the dog-eared book and dialed again. This scenario came to pass twice more. Today was the final day of school before the holiday break. There was a high school Christmas party tonight, and all of their regular sitters were previously engaged either in the childcare field or attending the party themselves. It didn't look good for Bill and Libby's planned outing. In desperation Libby dialed her next-door neighbor. The Johnsons were relatively new to the area, but Barbara had been Mike's babysitter one other time in the past.

"Hello, you've got the Johnsons."

"Hi, Bobby, Libby here. If you're not too busy come on over for coffee."

"Love to. Be there in a minute," came the reply.

Libby threw out the tiny bit of remaining coffee and put together a fresh pot. She wrapped two more presents for Mike and then the back doorbell rang.

"It's open," Libby called over her shoulder.

"Hi, Elizabeth. Wow, it's cold out there this morning." The visitor shivered slightly and hugged herself tightly against the chill. "Windy too."

"Should have worn your coat or at least a sweater," Libby remarked. "Coffee'll be ready in a minute."

"A coat? That's a good afterthought." The woman laughed, stretching her hands out above the gurgling coffee machine.

"Put a finger on this for me," Libby suggested as she labored to tie a fancy ribbon on a package. The bow was tied and the coffee poured a few minutes later, and the two settled down at the table.

"I've got a big favor to ask of you, Bobby. This is Bill's and my anniversary. We were going out for the evening, but I can't find a sitter for Mike. Could you…"

"Go no further. I'd love to. How long have you guys been married?"

"This is number ten for us. We tied the knot back in '88."

"Carl and I have been at it since '82. I've got you by six. How'd you and Bill meet?"

"Oh, I had my own apartment and was working for Henderson/Applebetz up in Philly. Bill got his law degree and came to work for them as a junior partner. We started dating and one thing just led to another."

Barbara winked and a quick grin crossed her features. "You mean Mike?"

Libby chuckled. "Yes. Oh, Bill and I were pretty sure right from the start so we weren't as careful as we should have been. We really didn't want to get married that early, but when I got pregnant we said "great" and went ahead and tied the knot. We settled down here in Bosway because of the rural atmosphere, the country living, the fresh air, and all of that. The commute for Bill isn't too bad. He drives down to the bus depot in town and he's at work in the city in just about an hour."

"Where's Bill from originally? I've caught a slight accent when he speaks."

"He's from Topeka, Kansas. Grew up there. He went to the University of Pennsylvania in Philly and then through their law school."

"You moved here from Colorado years ago, right?"

"Montana actually. I was nineteen years old, fresh out of high school, and searching for a fresh start."

Bobby rose and added a little coffee to her cup. "What on earth prompted you to come way back here to the East Coast?"

"Actually it was an accident. I was trying to get away from a bad home setting."

"What was wrong with your home, if I'm not getting to inquisitive?"

"Mom had died when I was seven. Following her death my dad's drinking slowly got out of hand. By the time I was in high school

I found him pretty obnoxious to live with. Still, he was quite decent to me. He paid me minimum wage to work the resort with him, and I saved most of it. My dad kept trying to borrow money from me, but I refused. I put up with it all the way through school, but after graduation I just couldn't take any more of him, packed up, and left.

Coming here was really an accident. I was on my way to Cleveland, Ohio, from Chicago, but I got on the wrong bus and found myself heading for Philly. I just figured that it was fate leading me on toward some sort of predestined life. I paid the extra fare and kept going.

When I got to Philly I found a small apartment, got me a cashier's job in a small deli, and took a crash course for a legal secretary's rating. I'd been really good at typing and all those computer skills they shoved at me in regular school, so it didn't take me too long to qualify."

"You don't work at all anymore, do you?"

"Oh, I help Bill out now and then when he has a big workload, and especially if one of the secretaries is out for some reason. The Internet makes it easy. I keep in practice."

"About tonight?" Bobby asked.

"Yes, Bill should be home by about six. I'll fix Mike his supper. He'll probably have some small amount of homework to do and then we let him watch TV till nine. That's bedtime for him. I'd guess Bill and I will be home before midnight. That sound all right to you?"

Bobby rose from her chair. "No problem. I'll feed Carl early. But right now, Libby, I've got to get going. I'm off to the library to pick up some books on needle craft. You know anything about needle craft?"

Libby laughed. "Sorry, that's one field I know nothing about."

The women parted company a few minutes later, and Libby took Skipper for a session at the dog-grooming parlor. While the little sheltie was becoming beautiful for the holiday season, Libby toured the small business district and bought a few more stocking stuffers for her family. Close to noon she dropped by the fitness center, showed her annual membership card, and plunged into a vigorous one-hour routine guaranteed to keep her in shape. She picked up the dog after this and was back home in plenty of time to greet Mike when he came in from school.

The latch clicked and the front door thumped shut. "Hi, Mom. I'm home."

"In the kitchen, but don't peek. I'll be done in a minute." Libby finished her last package and gave the all clear. "OK, Mike. You can come in now."

Mike walked quietly into the room, turned a chair away from the table and sat down straddling the seat. He folded his arms across the back. "What's in the package?" he asked nodding toward the brightly wrapped gift.

Libby laughed. "Wouldn't you like to know? Want to play twenty questions to find out?"

"Not with you. You cheat every time."

Libby ignored her son's barb. "How'd your last day of school go?"

Mike grimaced. "Terrible like all the rest. The teacher moved one of those rowdy kids right next to me. He's a real bummer of a creep. You should hear the things he keeps saying under his breath. At least school's out till after New Year's. I hate that damned school!"

Libby wagged her finger in warning. "Watch your language, young man, or you'll be sounding just like those other kids."

"I'm sorry, but I really hate having to go to that school."

"Your dad and I are working on a plan to send you to a private school beginning next spring. It's close enough that you can take the city bus back and forth and live at home as usual. It should be great for your morale. For now, just work hard, grit your teeth, and try to keep your grades up like you always have."

"I will." Mike swung out of his chair, crossed the kitchen, and began pulling dishes from the cabinet on the far wall.

"Hold it, Mike. Just set a place for you. Your dad and I are going out for the evening."

"Why? What's up?"

"It's our anniversary. Ten years ago today we were married. I've got a babysitter for you."

"Betty going to babysit for me again?" There was a short pause and then Mike snapped. "Oh, I hate that word, babysit."

Libby laughed. "No, honey, Betty's somewhere else tonight. Mrs. Johnson, next door, is going to keep you company. And you're right; I don't hire babysitters anymore."

"That's all right, I guess. I like Mrs. Johnson. I beat her at pinochle last time she was here."

Libby smiled as she removed the shambles left over from her wrapping project, and Mike set the table for one. Libby thawed out some Thanksgiving turkey and began putting together a bunch of leftovers for Mike's supper. She added some Stove Top Dressing and an ample serving of frozen green peas.

While all this was heating up Libby retired to her bedroom and changed clothes for the evening. As Bill suggested she pulled on a pair of jeans, choosing a tight-fitting pair of old faded ones that she particularly liked. A long-sleeved, light blue cotton jersey topped out her outfit, and she chose a Levi vest to wear over her warm jersey. She glanced once at her discarded loafers and turned to the closet for an alternative. It took a minute of digging, but she finally found her seldom worn, very old, extremely battered cowboy boots that she had kept ever since her days in Montana had come to a close. Every time she wore them she was amazed that they still fit. Libby pulled the cuffs of her jeans down over the top of her boots, looked in the full-length mirror on the back of her bedroom door, and saw that she looked great. Libby tipped the scales at 150 pounds, but her large frame and height of five feet eight inches carried the weight well. She quickly recognized the signs of radiant strength and the allure of a trim, well-toned body. It was really hard to believe that thirty-one years had somehow passed into memory.

In the bathroom she paused before the bright mirror and opened her makeup case containing all sorts of ingredients designed to correct what she perceived as her aging appearance. Libby seldom used any of these socially acceptable items, but for tonight she chose a light shade of eye shadow and leaning toward the reflecting glass surface started to apply just a touch.

Suddenly Libby shook her head. "To hell with this," she muttered, snapped the case closed, and returned it to the bottom drawer below the sink.

Back in the kitchen she stirred Mike's supper and glanced at the clock on the stove. It was dark outside by now, and the clock showed nearly 6:00.

"Supper ready, Mom?" Mike asked from the doorway.

"Sit down. I'll dish it up for you."

Just then bright headlights flashed across the kitchen window as Bill drove into the yard. Instead of driving into the big detached garage, designed to resemble a farmer's barn, he parked by the front door. Above the barn's two-car garage, in what was once the haymow, was a quiet office area where Bill spent some private time. He entered the house as Libby dished up her son's supper. Libby placed what was left of the food in a small bowl and platter on the table.

"Hi, honey" Libby called as Bill came into the small entryway. He hung his topcoat on a clothes tree and began loosening his tie as he moved into the kitchen.

"My, but you look great. Not a day over twenty, I'd guess… Hi, Michael. How was school today?"

Libby interrupted. "Don't ask him that."

"Bad day again, I take it."

Mike paused between mouthfuls. "You guessed it, Dad. I hate that place. It's like a zoo."

"Hang in there, kid. I think we'll get you out of there come the beginning of the new school year."

"Oh, I hope so. You know Mom's really not twenty, don't you, Dad?"

"Sure. I was just joking with her, but she looks remarkably good, don't you agree?"

"She's always just my mom to me," Mike explained.

Bill slipped out of his suit coat. "I'm going to change clothes and try to get comfortable. With a little luck I can look as young as your mother. Be back in a little."

"You two flatter a person to no end," Libby said as the back doorbell rang. Bill turned toward the rear door, just as it swung open under Bobby Johnson's hand.

"Hi, everybody," she greeted. She laid a heavy three-cell flashlight on the counter and, shedding her jacket, hung it across the back of a kitchen chair. Bobby slipped into a seat at the table and snitched a piece of hot turkey from the small platter in front of Mike.

Mike started to rise. "Want a plate, Mrs. Johnson?" he asked.

Bobby laughed. "Oh no, just sampling your supper." She licked her fingers, nodding her approval. "Good."

Bill retired to the bedroom without comment and returned a short time later. He had slipped into Levis and a plaid sport shirt with a bolo tie. Over this he wore a double-breasted sports jacket. He looked great and standing side by side with his wife they became an intriguing couple. Cell phone numbers were exchanged with Bobby, and the evening plans were laid out in general terms. By 6:15 the couple was ready to leave.

They slipped into Bill's Buick Rainier and headed for town. They wouldn't take the long drive into Philadelphia, choosing instead to party in the smaller rural villages south of the city. They stopped at one of their old time favorite restaurants and had a great prime-rib dinner that was well suited for any special occasion. Following their meal, and a splendid bottle of wine, they spent about an hour Christmas shopping in a mall decorated to the hilt for the holiday season. Christmas carols and the jingling of Salvation Army Santas' bells filled the air. It was a festive night filled with laughing children and shoppers deeply engrossed in the Christmas spirit of giving.

As they drove across town Libby broke the silence. "I hate this car of yours," she exclaimed.

"Why?"

"Darn bucket seats. We should have driven my old pickup with bench-type seats. I like to cuddle up with you."

Bill laughed as he reached across the console and squeezed his wife's hand. They pulled in at the Sundown Roller Rink a few minutes later. Over the years they had been here several times. In the beginning they struggled through the black and blue phase, but soon caught onto the activity. Even Michael, way back when he was only five, had taken to eight wheels without difficulty and very soon outshone his parents on the floor.

From the parking lot the strains of organ music could be heard. The swing and sway of dance music grew louder as they entered and joined the small crowd of skaters. Arm in arm they circled the arena. Forward and back they glided, round and round they spun. They were outnumbered greatly by the younger teenage set. Yet there were two other couples that were definitely in the senior class outdistancing them in both skill and age by many years.

At the snack bar they had coffee and their favorite coconut cream pie. Sitting at their little table they recounted their past years together.

"It's been hard, hasn't it?" Bill asked at one point, reaching across the table and gripping Libby's hand for a moment.

Libby smiled. "What do you mean?"

"Oh, I know you don't really like living here. I can tell that you're homesick for Montana most of the time."

"That's true, Bill. I really have never belonged here. Sometimes I am homesick, but my place is with you. Nights like this make up for a lot of the other times."

"You really hate the formal get-togethers, don't you?"

"Yes! Those office parties, the country club, the high-class client dinners, all of that. It's just so much pretense." Libby grimaced at the thoughts.

"But, it's all part of the game."

"You ever think of practicing in Montana?" Libby asked pointedly.

"Yes, but I've never really checked into it. I'd have to do some studying, and pass the Montana Bar, but it could be done."

"But you don't want to do it, do you?"

"Frankly, no," Bill admitted.

"The closest I come to Montana back here is in the spring and summer when I have my vegetable garden going."

"Yes I know. You practically live among the corn stalks and tomato plants."

"I love the feeling of the sweet damp earth. I love to feel it cool and wet against the knees of my jeans. It feels good ground into my hands. It would be such a great life for Michael out there." There was a long interval of silence while they sipped their coffee and watched the other skaters.

"The school system here worries me, Libby. There's just too much racism, too many ethnic problems, too much politics. I've thought about relocating for your sake and for his several times. But then I think about how far I've come with the firm, and it scares me to think about starting all over again. If Mike's new school doesn't work out next year, I'll bite the bullet. I'll be thinking seriously of moving."

Libby smiled. "And in the meantime I'll just grin and bear it. Going back home would be great, but regardless I'm with you for the duration. Come on, let's dance."

They rolled out onto the polished boards, locked arms front and back, and fell in with the circling crowd. It was an enjoyable two hours that slipped by. But then, as the bright neon clock on the rink wall showed 11:00 p.m., they headed for home.

The dancing beam of Bobby Johnson's flashlight lit the way as Bill walked with her across the tree-studded acre to her home. When he returned he found Libby fixing good stiff nightcaps for them both. They sipped their drinks and sat quietly in the living room admiring their tree and the other decorations. They cuddled quietly allowing their amorous spirits to get completely out of hand. At last they finished their drinks, turned off the lights, and retired to the warmth and security of their bedroom.

The following day Bill busied himself in his quaint office in the haymow while Libby and Mike demolished the kitchen baking three pies and four different batches of cookies. It was a tiring day, but lots of fun as well.

On Christmas Eve they all went to church for the short Christmas Pageant and service. It rained throughout the night, and Christmas itself turned out to be a blustery, cold, rainy day. It was far removed from what most people would envision for the holiday, and it made a liar out of the weatherman who had promised snow.

Libby's ham and other traditional goodies filled the house with their tantalizing fragrances. Mike's allowance had been tastefully spent on several worthy gifts for his parents and they in turn had shared their bounty with him. Late in the afternoon, an older couple from their church joined them for dinner; and as darkness descended the rain changed to snow. A little tardy for Santa's Chargers, but welcomed nevertheless. By seven o'clock almost three inches of snow blanketed everything, and everyone's appetite had been adequately satisfied.

Their dinner guests left just after seven; and the entire Emerson family, even little Skipper, bundled up warn and secure and went for at least a two-mile walk through the snowy, rural countryside. Above the gray overcast there was obviously a moon, and its brilliance struggled through the clouds just enough to light the magical scene. Neighborhood houses glistened brightly with festive decorations, and lights of many colors reflected off the carpet of unbroken snow. It was a beautiful evening, one that would never be totally forgotten.

CHAPTER II
Why
December 26–January 19, 1999

The rest of the week went by quickly. Bill was back to his regular commute, Mike spent many hours with the other neighborhood children sledding on the small hill behind the house, and Libby tended to her routine chores as usual. Bill was home early on Thursday night, as the office shut down ahead of time for a long New Year's celebration. Carl and Bobby Johnson joined the Emersons on Monday night as the two families welcomed in the New Year, 1999. Mike struggled with sleepy eyes to make it through the evening, but with Skipper's help, he managed.

Early January showed Michael back to his school routine. Libby attacked her holiday decorations, gently stowing everything away until next year. The tree decorations took one entire day to pack carefully away. By the middle of the month things were back to normal. On Monday the nineteenth Libby got her crew off to their separate workplaces and then she attended a lengthy meeting of a woman's group at her church. She was back home by mid afternoon and set about the early preparations for their evening meal. With the roast in the oven she settled down on the sofa, began reading the latest issue of *Time* magazine, and then dozed off.

Suddenly the doorbell rang. Libby's eyes popped open instantly, and she glanced at the clock on the mantel. A look of surprise spread across her face. It was too early for Mike, and besides, he had his own key. Libby swung off the couch and answered the bell. She opened the heavy door and in surprise confronted a county police officer standing there. The deputy was an older woman, very attractive, her short auburn hairdo quite gray at the temples. The officer was holding her hat nervously in one hand.

"Yes?" Libby began. She could feel the adrenaline surge through her body as she waited apprehensively for the officer's reply.

There was a moment of nervous hesitation. The officer cleared her throat. "Are you Elizabeth Emerson?"

Libby nodded slowly. "Yes." Her eyebrows knit together.

"Mrs. William Emerson?" the deputy asked, glancing at a small notepad in her hand.

Libby nodded again as she felt her knees begin to tremble and a strange knot suddenly clutched at her throat.

"Mrs. Emerson, may I come in? Maybe we could sit down together for a few minutes."

Libby shook her head and stood her ground blocking the open doorway.

The officer shrugged. "Mrs. Emerson... I'm sorry, but there's been an accident... A very bad accident."

Libby tried to speak, but her voice froze in her throat. She clutched at the door casing with one hand to steady herself as visions of her family spun crazily though her mind.

"It's your husband, ma'am. They just notified us from up in Philly."

Libby choked as she tried again to speak and just stared at the officer. She forced her eyes to focus on the department emblem on the shoulder of the officer's jacket as she waited for the woman to continue.

"I'm so sorry... There's no easy way to say this." There was a very long pause with nothing but silence surrounding them. "Your husband is dead, ma'am... I'm so sorry."

Tears began to flood Libby's eyes. She blinked hard trying to retain control, and the tears began to wash down across her cheeks. "No!" Libby gasped shaking her head vigorously... "How?" she asked. Her voice was nothing but a broken, disoriented whisper.

"He was in a building apparently reading some documents as he waited for an elevator. The elevator door opened, and he just stepped in..."

"And?"

"He fell... There was no elevator there. The controls had malfunctioned or something. I really don't know all the details."

The silence hung suspended around them for a long moment. "Is there anyone here with you?" the deputy inquired.

Libby just shook her head.

"Can I call someone for you?" she asked. "A friend, a neighbor, your pastor?"

Again Libby just shook her head in numb silence. The officer reached into the inside pocket of her jacket and produced an official business card. She slipped the card into Libby's hand. Libby saw tears in the woman's eyes as she passed the card to her.

"If there's anything I can do, anything I can do for you, if you just need someone to talk to, please give me a call."

Libby stood frozen unable to speak much less comprehend.

The officer finally turned very slowly away and moved down the short walk toward her car. Libby stood motionless in the open doorway for what seemed like hours. The car vanished into the countryside, and she was left alone with her grief. She finally closed the door and turned slowly to face her empty living room, her empty life. She clenched her fists at her side crushing the small business card as she did so. Then she threw her head back and let out a single, long, desperate scream of anguish.

It was silent then. Libby paced back and forth through the rooms of her home for endless minutes, and then she went to the kitchen where she poured herself a cold cup of coffee. She placed it on the kitchen table and stood staring down at the shimmering surface of the brew. What she had just heard could not be, it was all a mistake, it must not be true. Libby went to the sink, and washed her face with cold water. She was heedless of the water splashing down the front of her blouse. She settled down numbly at the table and sipped the cold coffee in utter silence. Sometime later Michael found her sitting there the empty cup before her.

"Hi, Mom. I'm home," he greeted cheerfully as he reached down to pat Skipper's furry head. "What's for supper?"

"A roast," was all Libby managed to blurt out.

Mike turned to the dish cabinet and began selecting what he figured would be needed for their coming meal. "The teacher moved that character again today," Mike said.

"I'm glad, honey. Just set two places tonight." Libby choked as she completed her short sentence.

Mike paused. "Dad's not coming?" He stopped and looked closely at his mother. "What's the matter, Mom?" he asked as he set the handful of plates down on the table.

Tears flooded Libby's eyes again, and with an open sob she grabbed Mike around the waist and pulled him into her arms. Mike sensed his mother's uncontrolled, open grief. It was contagious; and although in complete ignorance, he began to cry as well. They clung to each other almost in desperation for long moments. Finally Libby gained a measure of control, and she pushed Mike back far enough that she could look deep into his eyes.

"Sit down, Mike," Libby ordered swinging a chair back from the table with her foot.

Mike frowned and took the offered seat. Libby's chin quivered slightly. "Your dad died this afternoon," she stated simply.

There was a long period of stillness and then Mike melted into his mother's arms again, and they both wept openly. The phone rang several minutes later, and Libby was forced to begin the long flood of communications that was to follow. Mike, wearing no coat or hat, took his little Sheltie and ran from the house. He wandered around in the snowy yard for many minutes while his mother struggled on the phone. Maybe a half an hour passed before Mike returned to the house and without comment set the kitchen table for two. Twice before supper the phone rang as the word slowly spread. When the meal was ready, Libby took the phone off the hook and joined her son at the table.

"How'd it happen?" Mike suddenly asked while toying absently with his food.

Libby explained as best she could, and Mike simply nodded in mute understanding. Her information was sketchy to say the least. The whole thing was so bizarre, so incredulous a happening, that it defied description and logic. Both of Bill's law partners had called and the senior member of the firm, Eric Applebetz, was coming by the house in the morning. His instructions were to try to get a good night's sleep and not to worry. The firm would handle everything for her.

CHAPTER III
Pro Bono Publico
January 20, 1999

Libby was on the phone several times during the evening. Bobby Johnson came by and spent several comforting minutes with them both. Mike professed, "no homework tonight," and spent the evening in his room sketching ships at sea with his stereo set playing country-western music in the background. The walls of Mike's room held several pieces of artwork that he had done, all of them of sailing ships at sea. Trouble at school would usually produce another clipper rounding the Horn.

Libby turned off her cell phone, laid the handset of the house phone on the desk, and flopped down on the couch to rest. Only the small desk lamp in the corner of the room was left burning. It was 9:05 when she heard the flushing of the toilet and from the corner of her eye saw the ceiling light go out in Mike's room. Mike came across the dim living room slowly, almost with an air of uncertainty. He was barefoot, wearing only his jeans. He stopped by the couch and silently looked down at his mom. Then very slowly he sat down beside her.

Mike reached down and placed his hand on Libby's arm. "You all right, Mom?" he asked.

Libby wrapped her arm about her son's waist and hugged him closely. "No, Mike. I'm not all right, but I'm holding on."

"Why did this have to happen to us?" Mike questioned.

Libby swallowed hard as she tried to formulate an adequate reply. She choked on her words as she tried to answer, squeezed her son tighter, and made no reply.

"When Mr. Sutton died, Dad said that things like that just happen. It had something to do with God's will."

"I guess maybe your dad was right, Mike. Some happenings don't always have a good reason."

They rested silently together for several minutes in the semidarkness. Mike finally slipped from his mother's grasp and rose. He bent down and kissed her forehead lightly. "I've got to get to bed, Mom. School day tomorrow, don't forget."

"You don't need to go, if you're not up to it."

"I think I should. Dad said to work hard and keep my grades up. But I'll stay home if I can help you."

Libby smiled weakly. "You're a good boy… Thanks, but I'll be all right. In your prayers, Mike, just ask God for the strength and wisdom to see us both through this crisis. I know He will help." There was a long pause, and then Mike turned slowly away. "Night, Mike," Libby whispered.

The desk lamp went out in Mike's room and the door swung closed. Libby rested for maybe another half hour and then she rose from the couch. She paused uncertainly at Mike's room and then carefully opened the door. It was dark and quiet. Libby crossed to the bed and for the first time in several years leaned down and kissed her son's cheek. Mike didn't stir. His shallow, gasping breaths were a telltale sign of his stifled grief. He was obviously struggling with sleep.

"Call me if you need me, Mike," Libby whispered. In the darkness Mike's fingers closed briefly on Libby's arm as she turned away.

Libby didn't undress. She kicked off her loafers and crawled under the covers of her bed fully clothed. After an hour of tossing and turning, she finally became convinced that being the sole occupant of the bed, on this particular night, was not going to work. She rose, wrapped the bedspread tightly about her shoulders, and flopped down once more on the living room couch. Mike found her there the following morning.

Mike fed Skipper while Libby prepared their breakfast. They didn't talk much at all, and Mike was still planning to attend school. Libby faced an uncertain day up until ten o'clock when Eric Applebetz was due to come by.

She stood by the sink and watched as her son boarded his bus. Just as the bus pulled away a county police cruiser turned into their drive and approached the house. Libby recognized the officer that had delivered the terrible news the day before, and she turned and walked to the front door. Libby opened the door before the doorbell rang and greeted the officer.

"Remember me, Mrs. Emerson? I was here yesterday. I'm Deborah Newman," the deputy began.

"Yes. I remember. Please come in. I'm sorry I didn't have you in yesterday, but…"

"Don't mention it." The deputy removed her hat and entered the house.

Libby turned toward the kitchen. "Coffee?" she invited.

"Thanks. If it's already made."

Libby poured the officer a cupful and refreshed her own. "Cream or sugar?" she asked.

"Just black will be fine… You doing all right, Mrs. Emerson?' she asked crossing the room to the small kitchen table. She laid her hat and a large manila envelope on the table as she seated herself.

"Please. Just call me Libby. I detest formality."

"I know how you feel."

Libby took her seat. "Considering everything, I guess I'm doing as well as can be expected, right now. Last night I was just in shock mostly. Right now? I'm mad as hell at the whole world." Libby chuckled halfheartedly.

The officer smiled in understanding. "This came in from Philly sometime last night…" The officer paused fingering the envelope. "Would you like your husband's things now?" she asked quietly.

Libby just nodded as she twisted around in her chair to face the deputy. The envelope slid across the table, and she slowly opened the flap and dumped the contents onto the surface. There was a billfold, a Masonic tie clasp, house keys, a small handful of loose change, a money clip with several bills, car keys, a small notepad, a pair of fingernail clippers, and several pens and pencils. An official Philadelphia Police Department form listing the items was included.

Newman pulled a pen from her shirt pocket and extended it to Libby. "Please sign right there at the bottom and date it for me."

Libby nodded, ignored the offered pen, and signed using Bill's pen from the pile of personal effects.

"I know it's real early, but have you any plans yet?" the officer asked.

"Well, Deborah. I think I'll move back to Montana." Libby's reply took her completely by surprise. She was shocked by the words that suddenly had just leapt from her mouth.

"That your home originally?" she asked.

"Yes, many years ago."

They chatted for several minutes and then the deputy rose apologetically. "Thanks for the coffee, Libby. Right now I've got to get going."

"You going back to town?" Libby asked.

"Yes. Can I get you something?"

"Could you take me to the bus depot? Bill left our car there when he took the bus to work."

"Glad to. It's right on my way."

Libby jumped up, grabbed Bill's car keys from the table, and from the wall beside the back door picked up her coat. She snatched her billfold from the desk, locked up, and walked with the deputy to the car. The officer opened the passenger door and helped her get settled.

As Deborah Newman circled the car, Libby gave her surroundings a quick once-over. The officer settled down behind the wheel and buckled up. Libby ran her hand along the barrel of the pump action shotgun standing locked securely in a rack next to the console.

"Twelve gauge?" Libby asked.

"Yes."

Libby nodded. "Ithaca?"

"No, Browning, I think," Deborah replied.

As they drove down the road Libby turned to the driver. "This is the first time I've ever ridden in a police car," she stated. "You've even got your own computer."

"Yes, and I hope it's the last time you ever ride in one," Newman replied with a serious frown.

Next to the park-and-ride lot, Libby said her good-bye and climbed out. She thanked the officer for the lift and as the deputy pulled away began looking for their big Buick SUV. She located the car easily and within minutes was back home. She parked the Buick in the garage next to her little Chevy pickup.

As the saying goes, "she twiddled her thumbs," while she awaited her guest's arrival. Shortly before ten a taxi pulled into the drive.

Libby opened the front door and greeted her husband's boss as the vehicle pulled away.

"Come in, Mr. Applebetz," Libby began as she motioned for Bill's boss to enter.

"Please, just Eric. OK?"

Libby nodded. "My pleasure. First names all the way around." She closed the door and took Eric's coat as he slipped it from his shoulders. She hung the coat on Bill's clothes tree in the entryway.

As she turned back, Eric took her in his arms for a long, silent, hug of sympathy. Libby appreciated the moment, with some reluctance. Then, slipping from his grasp, she led the way to the kitchen. She had expected the man to arrive with a large briefcase full of documents, but he followed her to the table empty-handed. He sat down and from his inner suit coat pocket produced a single white envelope, which he placed on the table. Bill's personal effects were still resting there.

"Coffee?" Libby asked.

"Please, with cream if you have some."

It was quiet while Libby poured their cups. She placed the small carton of cream on the table and opened a Christmas cookie tin of assorted sweets. From a drawer beneath the counter she produced an ashtray, which she placed by Eric's elbow.

"You have a good memory, Elizabeth. Sure you won't mind?"

Libby smiled pleasantly. "I'll air out the room when you leave." She dropped into her seat. "It won't bother me."

Eric produced a sterling cigarette case, withdrew a cigarette, and snapped his lighter open. He blew a thin wisp of smoke toward the ceiling and opened the envelope lying before him.

"This is Bill's last will and testament. He filed a copy with us. Are you familiar with its provisions?"

"Yes."

"Bill named you as the executor, and I was named as the alternate. I certainly will leave it in your capable hands if you choose to handle it yourself, but I'd be glad to take care of everything for you."

"Well, Eric, you certainly know the ropes. It would be a big relief for me if you could handle all the paperwork. I imagine there will be lots of it."

"All right. I'd be glad to. There are mentions here of insurance policies naming you and your son, Michael as beneficiaries. Do you know where these policies might be?"

Libby shrugged. "I'd guess in the safe deposit box at the bank."

"OK… What about your home mortgage contract? Was it protected by insurance?"

"Yes. We were joint tenants, and all that stuff." Libby sipped at her coffee. "All those papers would be at the bank too."

"Outstanding debts?"

"Just a small credit card bill every month. Nothing much."

Eric withdrew a single sheet of paper from his jacket pocket and spread it out on the table. "This is a power of attorney form giving me the right to act on your behalf in any and all matters concerning your husband's estate. You will still have to sign any documents that would be transferring ownership or title to any of your real properties." Libby picked up Bill's pen and signed the sheet.

"Have you been in contact with the funeral home as yet?"

Libby looked down at her folded hands. "No. Bill's dad and sister are coming out from Wichita. They should be here tonight. I'll work with them on all of that. I do know that he wanted to be cremated."

"All right. Just keep us all informed about the services. We'll all want to be there. I don't suppose that you have made any plans about your future have you?"

"No definite plans. I did blurt out that I was moving back to Montana… Maybe I will, but nothing's been set as yet."

"Well, I have a brother in Philly that's in the real estate business. If you decide to sell your home, I'll put you in touch with him for a guaranteed no-commission deal. He owes me several favors." Eric chuckled.

Libby shook her head. "Thank you, but right now I couldn't even consider selling."

"Of course not. I'm just referring to down the road, if you should ever decide to move west." Libby nodded her understanding.

"Is my checking account OK, and are my credit cards still usable?" Libby asked.

"I'll ensure that they are for you. Give me a deposit slip for your checking account and your credit card numbers for all your cards.

I'd like to have your safe-deposit box key too unless you would like to be there when I go through it."

"I've nothing in the box personally that I can think of. I'll get you the key."

Libby slipped from her chair and from the desk picked up her key ring. She separated the lock box key and handed it to Eric. She laid out three credit cards and her checkbook on the table before him. Eric removed a deposit slip from the checkbook and scribbled down the credit card data on the back of the envelope containing Bill's will.

"When do I pay you for your services? Would you like a down payment now?" Libby asked picking up her checkbook.

"You owe us nothing. This is all pro bono publico."

"Which means?"

"Free... It may not fit exactly the terms of 'pro bono publico,' but it's our way of saying thank you to Bill for the wonderful work he did for us and for being such a good friend. We'll take care of everything for you, Elizabeth. Any calls you receive and any documents that you get? You just refer them all to us. We'll handle it all. Under no circumstances sign anything unless it comes direct from me. Forward the document to us, or call me."

Libby nodded quietly. "Oh, Eric, thank you so much. This sure takes a big load off of my mind. Thank you so much." The lawyer tamped out his cigarette in the ashtray, and Libby reached across the table and gripped the lawyer's hand.

"I've got to be going, Libby. Can you call me a cab?"

"Sure thing." Libby rose, and from her desk phone dialed a taxi for her guest.

Eric Applebetz slipped into his topcoat and stood with Libby in the small entryway by the front door. He reached out and circled her shoulders with one arm and hugged her closely.

"Call me anytime at work or at home. Down the road we'll be handling your lawsuit too."

"What lawsuit?" Libby asked surprised.

"Wrongful death. We're already putting together the preliminaries for it."

"Who's suing who?" Libby asked.

"You'll be suing the building owner and the elevator company, it looks like. Maybe even the two technicians that were working on the system at the time of the accident. Michael will be able to sue as well. We'll see."

"Oh, I don't know about all of that, Eric."

"Don't bother your mind with any of that right now. Just get your feet back under you. Whatever happens it's 'pro bono,' remember that. Just bear in mind that you and your son have lost the breadwinner in your family, not to mention a wonderful husband and father."

A horn beeped in the driveway as the taxi arrived. Eric Applebetz took Libby by the shoulders, kissed her quickly on both cheeks, opened the door, and slipped out of the house. The cab departed a moment later; and Libby stood, almost in a daze, for several minutes gazing out across her spacious front yard.

CHAPTER IV
Early Grief
January 21–April 1, 1999

Jim Emerson and his daughter Eleanor had arrived safely. The hectic days that followed were depressing and exhausting. The phone rang incessantly it seemed, and there was a never-ending display of vehicles parked in their driveway. Libby had never met Bill's sister Eleanor before. It soon became evident that the two women had each found a caring and close companion in the other, and they would be able to help one another through the difficult times forced upon them. Eleanor stayed at the house, while Bill's father chose to stay in a nearby motel. Libby gave Jim the keys to her old pickup. This allowed the man the freedom to come and go as he pleased.

When Mike was not in school he spent most of his time with his grandfather. It was strange really. Except for Mike, Jim Emerson left the family quite alone. Eleanor, however, was always there as part of the immediate family.

The quiet hours before bedtime belonged to Libby and her son. Eleanor usually retired early, discretely leaving Libby and Mike a private interval during which they could be alone, a solitary time in which to openly grieve. These were the moments that they chose to share their sadness, to cry together, to question the reality of it all, and to seek the strength needed in the hours and days to come. At times these sessions dissolved into times of utter depression as mother and son sat silently staring at one another with muddled thoughts spinning crazily in their minds.

The entire family was together as they made the arrangements with the funeral home. As Bill would have wished simplicity was the rule. Bill had always been a practical man and an advocate of small family celebrations for whatever the occasion might be.

A dinner was scheduled following the short service at the church, and all were welcomed. A well-known local restaurant provided a buffet-type setting. They were given a small banquet room for the group and two waitresses were assigned exclusively to their crowd. Bill's father paid for, and hosted, the entire affair. One of Mike's best friends was there throughout the evening, and the two boys kept close company with Bill's father. Jim seemed almost to use the boys as a crutch, covering up the grief that he undoubtedly felt at the loss of his eldest son.

The service and the food were very satisfactory. Still, this dinner, this gathering of friends, lacked the warmth and informality that Libby clearly remembered being exhibited at the time of her mother's funeral back in Montana. That happening, although twenty-four years in the past, had leapt to the forefront in Libby's memories. Today Libby was found to be at the focal point of everyone's deepest concerns, just as she was so many years ago.

Mike was busy at school when Libby drove Bill's father and sister to the airport the day following the service. The distance involved and the less than desirable weather conditions ended up making it a full day's venture. When she arrived back home she found Mike already there and in the process of thawing out some frozen wieners for their supper.

"Where's your salad makings?" Libby asked.

Mike shrugged. "Wasn't gonna have any salad," the youngster replied quite seriously.

Libby didn't respond, but went to the fridge and began putting together the balance of their meal. She gritted her teeth and without comment allowed the wieners, wrapped in bacon, to remain as the main ingredient of their dinner.

Throughout the remainder of January and on into February Elizabeth received registered letters almost every week from Henderson/Applebetz up in Philadelphia. Many required a signature and overnight return mail. She understood the complexity of most of the issues; and when in doubt, a brief phone call settled the question.

Eleanor and Libby phoned each other frequently, keeping in touch with all that was happening in their lives. The empty chair at the table and the vacant right side of the bed still were difficult and ongoing sources of pain; however, Libby had outwardly tried to adjust to both of these situations. As far as she and Mike could see, their routine lives hadn't changed much. Still, they both found a giant internal void and the periods of sheer depression created by Bill's passing.

Libby found herself every evening, about six o'clock, watching and listening for the sound of Bill's car as he returned from work. She couldn't help it. It was a deep-rooted and instinctive vigil that she kept, and it always led to a depressing moment of truth. She usually managed to blink back the tear, swallow hard, and go about preparing their evening meal in silence.

Libby was surprised when she came face-to-face with the number of things that Mike and her husband had done together. She realized this as she began having to take Bill's place with Mike at occasional outside activities. With Bill absent from the scene, it quickly became evident how many things went wrong around the house that he had cared for in his own way. She had no idea that Mike had been his father's helper in so many different tasks. Libby found herself spending more and more time in the basement workshop, which, until now, had been Bill and Mike's hobby and work area. She found these new adventures educational, to a degree, and quite entertaining. For the first time in her life the mother/son relationship had been reversed. Libby was now learning things from her young son.

In early March Libby was balancing her checkbook and noted that no debit had been applied concerning their house mortgage. A credit was also being shown for the past month's payment. Eric was obviously carrying through on all his promises. Her mortgage contract and other pertinent papers, she could now place in her closed file.

Mike had begun receiving Social Security survivor's benefits, which Libby deposited every month into his new savings account. These payments, she found, would continue until he was eighteen. The Henderson/Applebetz name kept showing up in the deposit column of her checking account. They were passing on to her a percent of the incomes from the accounts and cases that Bill had been responsible for. Still it all wasn't quite enough to make ends meet. Each month Libby found that she had to dip into her savings for small amounts to carry them through. Still, her five-digit savings account balance, at least for now, provided a comfortable margin to keep them going.

"It won't last forever, Mike," Libby explained one evening as she finally balanced her account and made another small transfer of funds.

"Maybe we need to sell this big house," Mike suggested.

"I've thought about it. It is costly to keep it up."

"I guess my new school's out for next year now, isn't it, Mom?" Mike asked.

Libby hesitated for a long moment. "I really haven't even thought about that, Mike," she said. "You're probably right... But if we sell this big house and move into something smaller... Maybe, just maybe, we could still swing it."

"I can chip in a little," Mike offered.

"No. You keep your money in savings for your future."

It was quiet for a long time in the room. Libby still sat at her desk aimlessly surfing the Internet. She finally switched to her stored photo albums and digging deep into the electronic archives came up with old photos of her childhood home in Montana that she had scanned and saved. Mike suddenly saw the pictures from the corner of his eye and walked over to pause behind his mother's chair.

"That the ranch?" he asked, placing his hands on his mom's shoulders.

Libby looked back at her son. "Yes. That's your grandpa and that's me." As she named the people, she pointed with the cursor arrow to each one.

"How many cabins are there?" Mike questioned, gesturing to the new picture showing some of the buildings.

"That's the old lodge on the right and two of the other smaller cabins over here." Libby clicked her mouse several times advancing the slide-show. "This is the main house where I grew up. There are five small guest cabins in all."

"There's no cows or horses," Mike complained.

"When I was a kid there were. Dad inherited the ranch from his father who had made his money in the Butte copper mines years before. I can remember all those cows and calves. But the cattle business got bad and the folks sold some grazing land and started building guest-houses. I guess they thought it would be an easier way to make a living. Worked out pretty good for them for a while."

"What happened then?"

"The worst thing was when Mom died. Remember I told you about her getting sick one spring. It turned into viral pneumonia, and she died. It was the year that I was seven. Dad kinda went crazy after that. He started drinking too much and got into a lot of scrapes in town all the time. I'll say this much for him; he always paid his bills and was never mean to me. When Mom died he had an insurance settlement, and he paid off everything he owed on the place. Then he set out to drink up all the money that was left. I just couldn't take it anymore. After I got out of high school, I came here. I never went back… I never saw my dad again… His drinking ate up his liver, and he died back in 1989. He was only forty-five years old."

Mike shook his head. "Who owns the ranch now?" he asked.

Libby shrugged. "As far as I know, I do. Your dad has always paid the taxes and insurance every year on the place for me. We were going to sell it a couple of times, but always changed our minds."

"Let's move to the ranch," Mike blurted out.

"What?"

"Let's move to the ranch. You said it's yours, Mom. We could buy some cows and horses and have a cattle ranch."

Libby laughed and swiveled her chair away from the computer to look at her son. She saw the excitement in his eyes. Of late this had been a rare offering. A moment passed, and then she turned without comment back to her screen and began clicking the photos one by one through her childhood.

"How about it, Mom. I'd have a better school and everything."

"Don't count chickens before they hatch, Mike." There was a lengthy pause again. "Tell you what, son. I'll give it some good thought. No promises, but I'll think about it."

On April first Eric Applebetz dropped by unexpectedly one morning. Libby found him sitting on her front steps when she returned home from having coffee next door with Bobby Johnson.

"I'm sorry, Eric," she apologized. "Please come in."

Eric rose stiffly from the steps. "I tried your cell phone," he muttered.

"It's sitting on my desk," Libby explained with a flush of embarrassment flooding her face. They moved directly to the kitchen where Libby began fashioning a fresh pot of coffee.

"Any problems pop out of the woodwork for you?" Eric probed.

"No. You've sheltered us both from most difficulties." Libby leaned back comfortably against the counter and watched as Eric began shuffling papers in the depths of his briefcase.

"Sit down, Elizabeth, and listen carefully now." Applebetz pulled his cigarette case out. Libby produced his ashtray and then took her seat. Eric fired up his smoke and began. "I've completed everything concerning Bill's estate. Only two hurdles remain concerning his death." There was a long pause while he thumbed through the papers. At last he passed two documents across to Libby. Attached to each was a bright business-type check.

"Here's number one. The personal life insurance policies that Bill had have paid off. As you can see, the double indemnity clauses of both policies have raised the settlements considerably. Between you and Mike you have right at $1,500,000."

Libby gasped as she scanned the checks and documents. Eric smiled as he dug deeper into his briefcase.

The lawyer finally nodded. "I feel rather like Santa Claus this morning... Ah yes, here it is... I've been holding closed meetings with four different parties. Our firm put together a lawsuit that would be twofold. One would be for your future welfare, the other on Mike's behalf, loss of guidance, tutelage etc. of a parent. I scared the hell out of all of them with a figure of eight million." The lawyer chuckled. "That was back in February... We've been back and forth for weeks with offer after counteroffer. Last night they came through with an out-of-court proposal. They've made a settlement offer of three million." Eric glanced again at the sheet in his hand and flipped it across the table. He leaned back comfortably in his chair and drew deeply on his cigarette.

Libby was astonished and sat speechless for a long minute before reaching for the paper. She scanned its legal wording, briefly noting only the dollar amounts specified. "Three million dollars?" Libby whispered, and a little nervous trickle of laughter escaped her lips.

"We can go to court, and maybe if all goes well, we could get more. It's always possible, but it would also be a very lengthy process. Then there could be appeals of the ruling. Theoretically you could end up with less. This settlement is a sure thing. Cash on the barrelhead, so to speak."

"What do I have to do?"

Eric reached across and pointed at the document. "Sign on the dotted line, right below your typed name, and date it."

Libby picked up the pen that Eric had placed on the table and nervously scanned the document. She turned it slightly and poised the pen above the dotted line.

"Elizabeth?" Eric interrupted. "Would you feel more comfortable if you took all of this to another attorney, anyone you choose, and had him look it over?"

"No, Eric. I'm completely satisfied. I just never expected anything like this. Three million up front and that won't affect Mike's Social Security benefits or my survivor's benefits down the line or anything?"

"This is a cash settlement by the parties involved. It won't affect any of your other benefits. But you are signing away your right to sue them for more later on, or for any other reason concerning the accident."

"Yes, I understand that."

Libby stared at the sheet for another minute while Eric ground out his spent cigarette in the ashtray. He immediately fired up another. Finally, with a flourish, Libby signed her name, dated the document, and slid it back across the table to the lawyer.

"Thank you," he said. "There'll be a bank draft in your account within twenty-four hours. I'd go to a reputable investment broker. The one you and Bill always have used is all right. Choose your investments carefully and you'll be in good shape for many years to come. Of course, it all depends on the economy, but you understand all of that. The market's been on a slide for the past few months so there are a few pretty attractive bargains out there. The economy still could get a lot worse." Eric chuckled at his own prediction. "I lean toward highly rated, tax-free municipal bonds with good payment histories myself. But your financial advisor is the guy to listen to. Don't put all your eggs in one basket though," he cautioned.

Libby fixed lunch for the two of them. When all the questions had been asked and answered she called a cab for her guest. He left shortly, headed back to Philly, and Libby settled down at the table awaiting Mike's return from school.

CHAPTER V
Westward Ho
April 1– May 30, 1999

"Hi, Mom, I'm home," Mike called from the living room.

Libby was patient. She heard Mike stop in his bedroom and a minute later heard the toilet being flushed. She got out the cookie tin, with its bright Currier and Ives scene on the cover, and placed it on the table. It now contained nothing but store-bought cookies.

"Hi, Mom," Mike greeted again as he entered the kitchen and immediately grabbed the cookie tin. He dropped down in a chair and looked across the table at his mother for several minutes. "Lost your tongue?" he finally inquired.

Libby smiled broadly and shook her head, causing her long ponytail to dance in the late afternoon sunlight. "How was school today?" she asked.

Mike grimaced. "About the same as always," he complained. "It's a madhouse at times."

Libby nodded, quietly letting the suspense build between them. She shook her head again trying to shake off the feelings of indecision, the numb sense of shock that still hung over her since Eric's departure.

"About your new school," she began, watching her son's face for his reaction.

Mike's eyes brightened immediately, and he gave his mother his undivided attention. "You got it all figured out?" he asked with a smile spreading across his face.

Libby dropped her eyes to study her strong hands where they rested on the table. "Not exactly." She looked back up at Mike's now disappointed face. "Still want to move to Montana?"

Mike looked quickly right and left around the kitchen as though trying to locate the source of the words he had just heard. His forehead wrinkled and an overall puzzled look spread across his face. "Move?"

"I've been thinking a lot about it. We could, you know."

"To the ranch?" Mike asked.

"Yes."

Mike's grin spread ear to ear. "And a new school."

"Yes."

"And we'll buy some cows and horses and raise cattle."

Libby shook her head. "Probably not," she replied. "Maybe one or two. Remember it's a guest resort."

"Wouldn't it cost a lot of money to move way out there and get started and all?"

"That's no problem now."

"I thought it was tough getting along without Dad," Mike stated.

Libby froze for a moment at his words. "It is, Mike. Believe me it is… But as far as money goes, no more problems right now."

"What's changed?"

"Mr. Applebetz came by today, Mike. There was a lawsuit and the people that were responsible for the malfunctioning elevator and your dad's death have paid us some money. It's like they are saying they are sorry and all of that."

"How much money?" Mike inquired.

"Quite a bit. But I'm going to invest it in different things so it will be there for a long time. Those investments will provide some income for us, but we'll still have to make a living and live day to day all by our own hard work."

"On the ranch? Oh, boy! I'll help! We can do it, Mom!"

"Yes! I think maybe we can. Right now this is going to be our secret, OK? Let's not blab any of this around the school, or the neighborhood, promise?"

Mike turned serious. "All right, Mom. How much money did you say they sent us?"

"I didn't. But it was a lot. Let's just let it go at that for now. And that's not all! Your dad took out a life insurance policy with each of us as beneficiaries and we received that money today. I'm putting your share into your savings account tomorrow for you."

Mike nodded, grabbed several more cookies from the tin, and went out the back door. Libby watched as he swung onto his bike and headed down the long driveway toward the road.

The following week Libby spent almost two entire mornings with her stockbroker. Over the next few days her portfolio began to take shape. As Eric had suggested the eggs were distributed among several baskets. They left a comfortable cash balance that could be used for moving and getting the resort back on its feet.

When Mike returned from school on the fifteenth of April he found a big Ford pickup parked in front of the garage. The big rig had a topper covering the open bed of the truck for great weatherproof cargo hauling.

"Hi, Mom. I'm home," he greeted. "Whose truck by the garage?" he asked looking quickly about the living room.

Libby swung around from her desk. "It's ours," she stated. "I traded both of our vehicles for it today."

Mike scowled. "I liked dad's big Buick. Why'd you sell it?" he questioned.

"Well, in Montana that big SUV wouldn't be very useful. And we couldn't take two vehicles when we moved. We'll probably be towing a trailer with our things in it and that will be easier with this bigger truck. It's diesel powered, four-wheel drive, and has a heavy duty towing package. If you noticed it's a crew cab with a good backseat and four doors. It has everything and will be good on the long trip. They call it the Super-Duty. Around the ranch it'll be priceless, especially in the winter months."

"Does it snow much in Montana?" Mike asked.

Libby choked back a laugh. "You better believe it, young man. *Knee deep to a tall Comanche*, as the saying goes."

Mike laughed and measured with his hand at about a two-foot level. "Wow! Is the truck new?" he wanted to know.

"No, but it's this year's model with real low mileage. Looks and feels almost new and still has the full warranty."

"When do we leave?"

Libby pushed her chair back from her desk. "Patience. School doesn't get out till the nineteenth of June."

"Oh, Mom…"

"I'll check with the school and see if we can leave earlier. I'd like to get going on about the first of June. Give me time. I'll hopefully work out something."

By May first the garage was stacked high with strong cartons from the liquor store. Most were still empty, but a small pile was beginning to grow with the carefully taped and labeled boxes containing A to Z of their personal belongings. On the twenty-first of May, Mike came home from school at his usual time and joined his mom at the kitchen table. Libby slid a document across the table to him. Mike turned it over and scanned it briefly.

"What's this?" he asked.

"Your graduation certificate from the fifth grade. The principal and your teachers both agreed that you were far enough along that they would give you credit for the two weeks in June that you'd miss. You've got one more week to go then we're off and running."

The joy that was expressed in the small kitchen was indescribable. Within minutes Mike was seen carrying two empty cartons into his bedroom. Libby shrugged and gathered up a pair of unused boxes herself and began some additional packing.

On Monday morning, the twenty-fourth, there was a tandem axle Hertz trailer backed up to the garage. An auction company inventoried the home and the contract was signed and sealed. The house was listed with Eric Applebetz's brother up in Philly with almost a promise of a quick sale.

The house was beginning to look empty. The walls were devoid of pictures, the shelves free of knickknacks, and the cabinets bare. Closets were empty and the basement virtually clear of its normal clutter. The big trailer was almost full, and Libby hooked it behind her truck. She drove across town to an industrial truck weigh-in scale where she had the entire rig checked for compliance with the highway regulations. She passed the test with flying colors. She would be many pounds under the legal limit on her long cross-country journey.

Libby stopped at a local truck stop on her way home. Many big rigs sat in the parking lot, several with their diesels idling noisily. Libby approached a likely looking individual eating alone in a booth.

"Excuse me," she began. "Are you a truck driver?"

"Afraid not, little lady. That's my Harley-Davidson out front. You want to go for a whirl?"

Libby felt a slight flush creep into her face. "No thanks, my mistake, I'm sorry… Enjoy your lunch."

Libby turned away, scanned the room again, and fixed her gaze on an elderly man, quite nondescript in appearance, eating alone in a booth beside the front window. She approached the man and introduced herself.

"Excuse me. I'm Libby Emerson," she began. "Are you a truck driver?"

"I've been called that among other things. That's my tanker rig parked out front."

"Could I sit and talk with you while you eat your lunch?"

"This is my supper, lady," he replied. "But be my guest, if you want to chat. But I don't take passengers."

Libby laughed and slipped into the seat on the opposite side of the table. The waitress came by, and she ordered coffee.

"Well, friend," she began, "to begin with, I'm not hitchhiking. I'm heading for Montana in a few days. I'm driving a Ford, F350, diesel, 4 × 4, one-ton, crew cab pickup, towing a big twin axle Hertz trailer loaded with everything. The trailer's got electric brakes, and the truck's got a five-speed transmission and a heavy duty towing package. I weighed the rig today and I'm legal. How about giving me some tips on driving a trailer down the road."

The trucker laughed. "Go slow and easy to start with," the driver began. "Stick to the Intestates wherever you can." For the next hour Libby tried to absorb all the information and suggestions that the trucker made. She paid particular attention to the tips about handling the two-brake system that her rig was equipped with. She made several pencil notes when they talked about routes to follow and areas to avoid.

The waitress finally presented them both with their tickets. Libby quickly grabbed the trucker's tab as they prepared to leave. They scuffled politely over the two tabs, and the trucker won.

"Have a good trip, Miss Libby," he advised. "Good luck in your new adventure."

They shook hands in the parking lot, and at the last minute the driver turned back and swept Libby into his arms. He gave her a big hug and a kiss on each cheek in parting.

"Stay out of the passing lane," he advised just before swinging up into his cab.

Mike closed out his school year on Friday. The rest of that day and Saturday were a whirlwind of activity. On Saturday night, mother and son toured the house, room by room, closet by closet, cabinet by cabinet. All was in order. The final item loaded came from Libby's closet. It was the brass-bound, varnished box, containing the ceramic urn holding Bill's ashes.

They stood in the living room on Sunday morning with nothing but their rolled up sleeping bags under their arms. Mike began to cry first. He turned, and his mother wrapped her arms about his shoulders for a long moment. Then she too began to cry. They wept together for several moments while their little sheltie, Skipper, looked up at them in wonder. At last they stepped apart. Libby locked the front door for the last time, slipped the key into a preaddressed envelope, and dropped this into the outgoing mail rack. They each hesitated for several minutes in the cab of the truck.

"Buckle up, kid. Here we go," Libby finally ordered.

The heavy rig began to move down the long landscaped driveway. For the final time, they each glanced back at what had been home and security for them both for so many years.

CHAPTER VI
The Endless Road
May 30– June 10, 1999

Libby and Mike were out of the city limits by the time the sun rose behind them. Their first rest stop of the day was at an inviting restaurant at an interstate interchange. The loaded trailer was towing very well, and Libby was almost not aware of its presence. They had two extra West Coast mirrors attached to the front fenders of their truck so there was a good view at all times of what was going on behind them.

They had set their sights on Pittsburgh for their first day's travel. They would log a little over three hundred miles before stopping for the night. During the course of the day, Libby stopped briefly for rest area breaks and occasional weigh stations. At a small number of the weigh stations she was just waved on through. The big truck's twin fuel tanks gave them great freedom from stopping for fuel every now and then. Little Skipper was given a drink of water at the breaks and chose the opportunity to water the bushes at each rest stop they came to. He was a very good traveler. Close to noon they made a brief stop where they ordered burgers and milkshakes to go.

Mike was placed in charge of their small satellite navigation unit. He was well versed in its use and had used it many times in the past when his dad had been the driver on family outings. The younger generation seemed inherently well suited to the gadgetry of the twentieth century.

"In three-tenths of a mile exit right… Exit right… Continue fourteen miles," came the instructions.

"Dad says that that woman has a sexy voice. Do you think so?" Mike asked.

Libby choked back an open laugh. "That sounds like your dad. I guess that just depends."

"On what?" Mike wanted to know.

"That was just your dad talking. There's nothing to it at all."

Mike shrugged and opened a package of Ritz Crackers for a snack. He handed one to Skipper in the backseat and one to his mom. Libby leaned over slightly and took the cracker from his fingers with her lips.

They were close to Pittsburgh well before suppertime and Mike clicked in for motel information and read the satellite's choices to his mom as she drove along. The decision was made and the new destination set. A few minutes later they arrived. Libby parked by the motel office, registered, and then moved the rig to the assigned parking area. In the room she flopped down flat on her back across one of the double beds.

Mike turned on the TV and dropped down on the other bed with Skipper by his side. About a half hour passed before Libby moved. From the backseat of the truck she got her suitcase and travel bag and lugged them back to the room. She tossed the truck keys to her son.

"Go get your bag and bring in Skipper's food and his two dishes," she ordered. "Don't lock the keys up when you're done."

When Mike returned he found his mother in the shower. Libby was dressed some time later. She still wore the same old jeans, but had slipped on a fresh clean blouse. Mike showered next, and then they walked about a quarter of a mile to a small restaurant where they enjoyed an early supper.

Following the meal they spent some time going over the big road atlas that they carried. Tomorrow they would be out of Pennsylvania with their planned destination being Fort Wayne, Indiana. It would be a little longer trip than they had experienced today, about 360 miles in all.

They watched TV together for a while, and then took Skipper for a short constitutional. After this, Libby went into the bathroom, changed into her nightgown, and crawled into bed. Mike followed a few minutes later, switching the TV and room lights off before he turned in.

This was pretty much the way it was to go for the travelers in the days ahead. After Fort Wayne it was Peoria and then Des Moines. They were about halfway to Montana. Between Peoria and Des Moines Mike got a surprise as they crossed the Mississippi River.

"Thought it would be a lot bigger than it was," he exclaimed looking back over his shoulder.

The agricultural and rural countryside that surrounded them for most of their days was interesting in the beginning, but soon became monotonous to a degree. Mike's comment at one point was, "Corn, corn, corn. I'm sick of seeing fields of corn."

Sioux City, Iowa; Rapid City, South Dakota; and then Sheridan, Wyoming, clicked off behind them. At last they were crossing the plains and passing through cattle country.

North of Sheridan they stopped at the Little Bighorn Battlefield, where Custer made his renowned last stand. Mike spent so much time there that Libby knew that she would have difficulty making her destination at Missoula that day.

True, it was the longest leg of their journey, about 466 miles in all, and they would be slowed by the first of the major Rocky Mountain passes. Mike was agog when he awoke from a brief nap just west of Livingston, Montana, and saw ahead of them the first of the snow-capped peaks that seemed to be blocking their path.

They climbed through the mountains in company with many slow-moving semis. The scenery was spectacular, and Mike's running comments were much better than any radio entertainment that they could have chosen. Libby pulled the visor of her ball cap down over her eyes as they chased the setting sun. It was almost dark when they reached Missoula, their next-to-the-last stopping point on their epic journey.

Mike closed the big atlas. "Only sixty-five more miles to go," he declared as he prepared for bed.

Libby didn't answer. She was fast asleep, fully clothed, face down across her bed. Mike pulled the covers of the bed down over her tired body, turned off the lights, and crawled under his own blankets.

CHAPTER VII
Home
June 11, 1999

They were off of the interstate now. The multilane throughway had been their home for over a week. This narrow state highway was a driving challenge to Libby, but she handled it and the heavier traffic like a veteran. For many miles they followed the North Fork of the Clamis River and finally entered the small town of Boder.

Libby pointed to the right side of the street. "That's where you'll be going to school." She indicated the modern building just off the main street of the sleepy town.

Mike craned his neck to look back. "It's not a very big school, is it," he stated as they drove by.

"Doesn't have to be big. There're not a lot of kids in comparison to what you've been used to."

"That where you went to school?"

"The part on the right is new since I went there, but yes, it's about the same, I guess."

They were through the small town in less than ten minutes. The road narrowed more, leaving only a narrow shoulder bordering the pavement, but it was still a good road as they moved farther up the valley. Their navigation unit suggested, "Turn right in three-tenths of a mile."

Libby disagreed. "No way! It's a better road up ahead. Just turn that thing off, Mike. Shoot, I don't need that sexy-voiced tour director here! Remember? I was born here!" Libby laughed.

They turned off the main highway, leaving the Clamis River, and began climbing gradually up a narrow, winding, paved road paralleling what was known as Gomas Creek. The stream could be seen easily off to their left through the tall trees. The crystal clear waters bubbled and boiled over the rocky streambed. At one point an old, rusty, steel truss bridge spanned the thirty-yard creek bed. It provided access to several log homes built on a long narrow shelf of land along the far side of the creek. The terrain rose steeply behind this small bench where the homes were located. Mike had to duck his head almost to the dashboard to catch a glimpse of the top of the ridge. This steep slope was dotted with a loose collection of stunted pines, none of which matched the grandeur of those old-growth trees crowding the fertile soil along the twisting pathway of the creek. The face of the ridge was covered with grass, weeds, and brush most already showing signs of the parched environment in which they were struggling to survive.

About six miles from the highway, Libby slowed to almost a crawl with her turn signals clicking. They rounded a tight bend in the roadway, and Mike saw the large dilapidated sign promoting, TANNER'S RESORT. The right-hand end of the sign had come unfastened from one of its tall legs leaving the sign hanging by one corner at a sharp angle.

Libby unfastened her seat belt. "Well, Mike, we're home at last," she announced as she turned off onto the unpaved Forest Service road.

"Where?" he asked, looking around at the tall timber that was flanking both sides of the narrow gravel road.

Libby gestured with her thumb, pointing to the rear. "Our property line is right back there at the highway. The house is just up ahead."

They came around a sharp curve, and Mike could now see a smaller course of water plunging down the gentle slope on the left side of the unpaved roadway.

"Is that the same creek?" Mike asked.

"No. That's the east fork of Gomas Creek. It joins the main creek a short way above where we just turned off."

Topping a little rise they came out of the trees and spotted the group of log buildings. The big lodge structure was quite prominent, as was the line of small cabins. Behind this collection of buildings, higher up along the open side of the small valley, Mike saw an older log home and several nondescript wood-sided barns and sheds. Many of these older buildings showed the lack of maintenance that they had endured over the passing years. Libby suddenly slammed on her brakes and stopped abruptly. A thin cloud of dust from the roadway caught up with them and swirled up about their truck.

Libby clicked her window down. "What the hell!" she muttered.

"What's wrong, Mom?"

"People, and cars." Libby gestured toward the complex. "What the hell's going on?" she wondered as she shifted into low gear.

They climbed the short hill from the main Forest Service road up to the resort proper. A bearded man came out of the first cabin, and Libby stopped as he approached. She instinctively checked her door-lock switch and poised her finger above the window control. The man wore open-toed sandals over his bare feet and one shoulder strap of his ragged bib overalls dangled from his waist. Beneath these overalls he wore a sleeveless grimy undershirt long overdue in the ragbag. He was quite bald and what remained of his halo of dark hair jutted out at frivolous angles from his head. He looked like he had just awakened and been ejected from the bed.

The man leaned against the side of the truck. You lost, lady?" he greeted.

Libby steeled her nerves and quite matter-of-factly replied, "Hardly. I happen to own this property. I live here."

The man pried the top off of a can of beer. "Never seen you before," he countered.

"Take my word for it, Mister. Just what the hell are you doing here? Are you some sort of a caretaker, or what? If so, who hired you?"

"Me? A caretaker?" The man laughed aloud, quite surprised at the thought, and spit a long stream of tobacco juice off to the side of the driveway. "You gotta be kidding."

"You're just a squatter then, I take it."

"Guess so, and we got our squatter's rights. Call us what you will. Me and two other families been living here for over a year now. Been lots of others come and go now and then since old man Tanner died. We call this place Peace Haven."

Their conversation had started to draw a small crowd. Three or four children had appeared, and two women, one of whom was obviously in the late stages of her pregnancy, were gathering about the truck.

"Well you don't live here anymore," Libby stated quite bluntly. "You're trespassing."

"Want to bet? We're settled here, lady; and we ain't goin' nowhere," the man stated belligerently. He took a quick sip of his beer and swallowed. How he managed this with a jaw full of chewing tobacco was more than Libby could fathom.

Libby gripped the steering wheel of her truck for several long silent moments as she faced the situation and counted slowly to ten. "Maybe we can work something out," she began, turning back to face the man. "I'll rent you one of the cabins in exchange for an honest day's work. There's lots that needs doing around here, I can already tell."

"I ain't no damned maintenance man, lady. This was abandoned property and we've moved in. We like it here. If you want to live here too, that'll be fine with us. We won't bother you. Just pick you a house and move in. We're using these first three. But stay the hell out of my way!" The man raked the cheek full of chewing tobacco from his mouth with a grimy finger and spit twice. He took a long swallow from his beer can, turned on his heel, and without further comment walked back toward the cabin.

Libby sat quietly for a moment, released her trailer brakes, eased out her clutch, and moved slowly up the hill toward the main house. She parked and shut off the engine.

"What do we do now, Mom?" Mike asked looking back down toward the cabins.

"Call in the cavalry," I guess." Libby pulled her cell-phone from its little case on her belt and very deliberately dialed, nine-one-one.

"Emergency operator," was the reply.

"This is Libby Emerson. I have just returned to my home out here on Gomas Creek, and I find that I have a bunch of trespassers, squatters, if you like, that have taken over the place and refuse to leave. Can I get some help out here?"

"I'll connect you with the Sheriff's Department. One moment please." The connection was made, and Libby explained her problem a second time.

"Would that be out at the old Tanner Resort?" the dispatcher asked.

"That's the place. I'm just moving back here from the East Coast and find that I've been overrun by squatters."

The dispatcher laughed. "We know the place. We've been interested in that bunch for some time. I'll send a deputy right out. Just stay put and leave them alone till he gets there."

Libby agreed and opened her door to get out. Little Skipper leaped from the cab and dashed off to water several small bushes as he explored his vast new empire. Libby led Mike across the narrow band of hard-packed dusty ground to the main house.

For the first time in over twelve years Libby moved slowly up the three steps and put her foot on the front porch of her old home. The deck extended the full width of the sturdy two-story log structure protected from sun, rain, and snow by a sturdy, cedar-shingled roof. The front door to the house stood open sagging on a broken hinge.

Libby pushed her way inside and paused, looking down the long central hallway toward the back door. This corridor divided the house into two nearly equal segments. The passageways, and the mudroom at the rear of the house, were covered with a heavy grade of indoor-outdoor carpet so threadbare that it would have to be replaced. The floor covering in the kitchen, bath, and laundry room was vinyl and long past being serviceable. The flooring in the rest of the house was of clear grain pine planks special ordered by her dad many years ago. These timbers were hewn from old-growth logs that he harvested on the ranch in those early years. Each board was of tongue and glove construction, twelve inches wide, and two inches thick. From what Libby could tell, all were in pretty good condition. A few scatter rugs here and there would make it begin to seem like home.

Unlike many modern log homes, the interior walls were not covered with expensive paneling. Instead they showed the rough hewn surface of the sturdy logs themselves, each heavily chinked to perfection. Libby's dad, in his younger years, had spared no amount of labor and love on this home's construction. It had functioned well for him and his family, and had surprisingly survived for the many years that it had been left unattended.

Libby turned to her left through an archway and froze facing the utter shambles of what had been the living room. The far side of the room was dominated by a huge cast-iron wood stove whose flickering eyes in the vented firebox door Libby remembered well from her childhood. All about the room were discarded pieces of broken furniture and other nondescript items, but nothing of a personal nature remained.

As her eyes adjusted to the dim interior she caught a hint of motion as something darted across the hall from the archway leading to the kitchen area. Skipper let out a shrill cry and dashed after the fleeing shadow as it vanished across the mudroom and through the doorway into the old master bedroom.

From the living room Libby turned right along a short hall and glanced into the wreckage of what had been her father's office. The rolltop desk was gone as were the filing cabinets and her dad's heavy leather desk chair. The small counter where guests were registered was the only tangible piece of furniture left in the room.

The next doorway led to her mother's sewing room in the corner of the house. It was now virtually empty of any furnishings. Directly across the hallway was the door to the laundry room. A quick glance showed that all the major commercial grade appliances were still there, but whether or not they were in workable condition was quite doubtful.

At the end of this small hallway there was another outside door leading to a small porch facing the old barn. Libby pushed this door open to allow more fresh air into the building. Everywhere she went she was plagued by the nauseatingly sweet stench of something dead, of garbage, mold, and mildew. No longer were there any lingering memories of the wonderful aromas of home baking, a well-prepared supper, or just the fragrance of strong honest everyday living. Libby almost wished that she could catch just a trace of her father's whisky-laden breath from somewhere within the walls.

Toward the back of the house she checked the kitchen and bath areas. Here as in the laundry, most of the major appliances were in place, but their serviceability was highly questionable. The large kitchen table and chairs were gone, giving the room a very naked and inhospitable air.

The floor in the incredibly filthy bathroom showed obvious water damage and was cluttered with trash. The master bedroom, in the back corner of the house, was devoid of any furniture. In a corner of one of the two closets Libby found the heap of sticks, leaves, and refuse that was one of the many pack rat nests that they would eventually find.

The mudroom, as her dad called it, was the rear entryway to the house; in the ranching days it was the primary point of access to the dwelling during the working day. It was a sizable room, better than twelve feet square. The east wall of the room held a double row of heavy wooden pegs set deep into the log wall for hanging coats and hats and below these was a rough-hewn bench of sorts. The rest of the wall space was taken up with counters containing cabinets both above and below. Most of these cabinet doors stood open, several hanging from broken hinges.

She only glanced up the flight of stairs toward the second floor. Heavy cobwebs stretched across the stairway daring her to intrude. The back door, like the front entryway had been knocked from its hinges and was simply leaning in a haphazard fashion against the opening. Libby pushed it outward with her foot allowing it to fall with a dusty crash onto the small back porch. This allowed more of the fresh mountain air into the house.

Many of the windows throughout the building had been smashed by vandals and would have to be replaced. All of the ceiling fixtures had been ripped out leaving only the dangling remnants of the electrical wires still in place. Libby went back to the porch and dropped down on the top step completely stunned by what she had seen and by the unfolding course of events. Surprisingly there were no tears, but her hands were shaking openly with pent-up anger.

Mike read his mother's mood. "We'll fix it all back up, Mom," he promised.

Libby just nodded. "Those bastards," she muttered.

"Don't cuss, Mom!"

"I'm sorry... You're right."

"Remember, Mom. You said it might be in really bad shape."

"Yes, I know, but I didn't expect anything like this. I guess I was pretty naïve. Let this be a lesson to both of us, Mike. You have to keep close tabs on anything that you wish to keep. That way you can reassess your position, and you will always have ongoing options concerning your actions."

Probably a half hour passed and then a county patrol car swung up along the creek. It paused by the cabins briefly, the driver spoke with two people for a moment, and then proceeded up the grade to the main house. The deputy parked behind Libby's big trailer, slipped from his car, and moved to the porch. Libby rose from the steps and stepped down to the ground to meet the officer. She extended her hand.

The officer slipped a small notebook into his shirt pocket. "Mrs. Emerson?' he greeted.

"Yes, but call me Libby." They gripped hands. "This is my son, Mike."

"I'm Deputy Taylor, Sheriff's Department." The officer shook Mike's hand and turned to look out over the resort. "You talked with them?" he asked.

"Yes." Libby pulled off her baseball cap and ran her fingers through her long dark hair. She went over the conversation that she had had with the trespasser and relayed the man's response.

"You want them out of here, no doubt?"

"I offered one of them a job in exchange for one of the cabins, but he didn't want it."

The deputy shook his head forcefully. "Don't hire any of them. That's wishing yourself into lots of trouble. Stay here a minute."

The deputy walked down the hill to the cabins. By the chevrons on the sleeves of his shirt, she took him to be a sergeant. He was a big man and carried himself in a very confident manner. He drew a sizable crowd almost immediately. Even from a hundred yards away, Libby could hear shreds of the heated discussion and the ensuing ultimatum. At last the officer turned and walked back up the slope to the main house. As he came up the hill Libby could see that he was talking on his hand-held radio with its mike clipped to the shoulder strap of his shirt. The deputy went to the steps and sat down quietly in the shade. Libby and Mike joined him.

"Now we just wait and see," the officer muttered. "I'm Gordon Taylor, by the way. Welcome to Montana." He chuckled ruefully.

"Wish I could be meeting you under a little different circumstances," Libby replied. "Did you go to school in Boder?"

"Sure did. Graduated in '83."

"Thought you looked familiar. I'm class of '85."

They talked for several minutes, even laughed together at times. Libby briefly went over her childhood here, her life on the East Coast, her husband's death, and their trip west. It came as a surprise to her at how quickly such a long period of time, over twelve years, could be brought to light.

All of a sudden three cruisers rolled up the Forest Service road. One stopped by the creek and turned sideways in the road blocking it completely. One of the remaining cruisers was a state Highway Patrol vehicle. The two cars proceeded up to the cabins one from either end of the circular drive.

Gordon Taylor rose, paused by his cruiser long enough to get his big shotgun from its rack, and all four officers converged on the startled group of transients milling aimlessly about the cabins. Red, blue, and amber, strobes were flashing, it seemed, everywhere. One of the deputies let a big German shepherd out of his cruiser, and the dog immediately began to bark and strain furiously at his heavy leash.

Libby held Skipper close by the porch with a curt voice command, "Skipper, stay!"

There was quite a ruckus for several minutes. Two of the belligerent men, including the one that Libby had spoken with, were lined up against a cabin wall and searched. Following a thirty-minute altercation, three people, including the pregnant woman, were handcuffed and placed in two of the cruisers. Heated discussions went on with the remainder of the group for several extended minutes; and then the posse, if you could call it that, all headed back to town. All, that is, except for Gordon Taylor who walked back up the hill to join Libby and her son on the front porch of the house. He returned his heavy gun to the rack in his car.

The deputy sat down. "They'll be out pretty quick," he announced. "If they don't go, we'll haul the rest of them off too."

"Did you arrest those people that you took in the cars?" Mike asked.

"Yes. Narcotics charges. Ted's dog went crazy, you saw that, I guess. He didn't even know where to begin searching," Gordon laughed. "You're not planning to stay out here tonight are you?"

Libby was defiant. "Hell, yes. I've got to look after everything, now that I'm back."

"You want to be careful around here. We're sending a team out, probably tomorrow, to go over the place, evidence gathering, you know.

We'll get all the dope and chemicals out of there for you, if there's any left, but be careful. We might miss something. If you want to file charges against any of them, just come by the office."

As they watched, the remaining people were busy loading the old cars and pickups that stood there. Soon, one by one, the trespassers drove away. As the last vehicle departed, Deputy Taylor walked back down and went cabin to cabin along the line and then swung through the spacious lodge building. When he returned to the house, he was satisfied.

"They're all gone, Mrs. Emerson. But, to put it mildly, I'm afraid you've been left with one hell of a mess."

"Yes, I know that… But it's Libby, remember?" She paused as her correction sank in. "It will take time, but we'll get it all straightened out," she promised.

"I'll drop by off and on and check on you folks. We'll have a spot check on all shifts for a few days to make sure none of that crowd comes back."

"That's nice of you guys. I can't begin to thank you enough for helping us out."

"That's why we're here… Have a good day, Libby. You too Mike. Glad to have met you both."

Gordon climbed into his cruiser, drove around the large circular roadway surrounding the resort, and headed back down the Forest Service road out of sight.

Libby and Mike toured the cabins and selected the cleanest one, the one with the least amount of structural damage, and started house cleaning. The cabin they chose was also one of the two that had a small wood stove for auxiliary heat and cooking.

Originally all of the cabins were essentially the same. Each had a single spacious bedroom. One additional large room served as both a living room and kitchen area. Between these two areas there had been small dining tables and chairs, most of which were now missing. Each of the cabins had been stocked with all of the essentials that guests would need for housekeeping—dishes, cooking pans, utensils, flatware, linen, and bedding, and even appliances. The major appliances hadn't worked ever since old Ed Tanner died, and the power had been turned off.

All of the television sets—each cabin had had its own—and all of the small electrical appliances were missing, probably stolen and hocked over the years. Most items made of fabric of any kind were green with mold and mildew.

Libby started a pile of useless items, from their selected cabin, on open ground between the main house and the other cabins. Everything from broken dishes, to mattresses, from cabinets, to pieces of furniture would be piled there to be burned at a future date. In the late afternoon hours they had the one cabin as ready as possible for their first night's stay.

It would be a primitive existence to say the least, as they had no running water and no electricity. There was water damage everywhere, especially in the bathrooms and kitchen areas. Plumbing fixtures including toilet bowls and tanks had frozen and ruptured during the bitter Montana winters that had slid by for nine full years since Ed Tanner had passed away.

The cracked toilet in their cabin was still marginally functional. However, one had to carry a bucket of water from the creek and pour it into the bowl each time after use. The underground septic system had apparently escaped any serious damage by the weather. About seven o'clock Libby blocked the wheels of her trailer and unhooked the rig from her pickup.

"Come on, Mike," she called. "Let's go get something to eat."

They climbed into the truck and took the thirty-minute drive down the valley to Boder where they parked on the wide main street. In the restaurant they were greeted by a pleasant enough waitress who strongly recommended their supper special. Libby thought the woman had a familiar look, but didn't pursue the matter of identity. As she and Mike waited for their meal an older woman approached their table from the kitchen area.

"Elizabeth?"

Libby turned to face her. "Yes, I'm Libby."

"Haven't seen you in many years. Remember me? I'm Dora Sanders. I own this joint now. Your mom and I were good friends."

"Of course. You had a son named…" Libby snapped her fingers and paused to think. "Daniel? Yes, Danny."

The woman nodded and frowned. "Danny died in a logging accident five years ago."

"I'm so sorry," Libby replied. "This is my son, Mike."

The owner and Mike shook hands. "You back to stay?" the woman asked.

Libby nodded. "Yes!"

"You going to reopen the lodge?"

"Yes. But it will take some time."

"Good to have you back again. Please come by and see me. Remember where I live?"

Libby thought for a brief moment. "East of town on the highway?"

"Right on." The waitress approached and Dora stepped back. "Enjoy your meal, Libby, tonight it's on the house."

After their supper Libby stopped at the small supermarket and bought some groceries that she could handle with no refrigeration and nothing but the small wood stove in the cabin. They were back home just before dark. Skipper made a beeline for the main house and scampered around, barking wildly, as he chased the horde of packrats that had decided to make the house their home. Down in their cabin row, Libby found very little evidence of the rodents and almost no broken windows. Possibly being occupied by the transient people had had a positive side after all. It had kept the packrats and vandals at bay.

They listened to Skipper's barking for well over an hour as he unsuccessfully pursued his quarry from room to room up at the main house. Mike gave a sidelong glance at the moldy surface of the couch's upholstery, shook his head, and finally unrolled his sleeping bag on the floor in the living area. Libby spread her sleeping bag over the box spring of the double bed rather than on the filthy surface of the mattress and just sat there in the gloom. It was almost totally dark when Mike began to breathe deeply from the other room.

Libby rose from the edge of her bed and quietly walked out into the chill of the Montana night world. Her feet took her down to the edge of the rattling creek and she paused to reflect on recent events. Skipper suddenly joined her. They sat silently on the creek bank watching the swift water rushing past. Libby's homecoming had been a far cry from what she had hoped for. In her mind whirled a kaleidoscope of a million chores that she was faced with, each struggling to become paramount on her lengthy list of priorities. It all seemed to loom as an impossible barrier to the dream that she had envisioned back in Bosway, Pennsylvania.

Just what was she expecting of her young enthusiastic son? Just what was she expecting of herself? She tipped her head back trying to focus through her tears on the brilliant star-studded sky above her. She cried long and loud almost in desperation. It helped. Nearly an hour had slipped by before she returned to the cabin and thankfully fell asleep on her makeshift bed.

CHAPTER VIII
Rebuilding
June 12– July 31, 1999

The rattle of the wood stove's door as Libby kindled her fire, broke into Mike's sleep the following morning. "What time is it?" he asked sleepily as he rolled over in his sleeping bag.

"After six," Libby replied, pausing as she put together a pot of coffee in a large saucepan that she had located in the back of one of the cabinets. There was no basket for the grounds and the whole thing would turn out to be like old-fashioned cowboy coffee at best.

Mike rolled from his covers and crossed to the window overlooking the meadow, the road, and the creek beyond. "Mom! Look there's deer in the yard."

Libby looked over Mike's shoulder. "Nope, those are elk. Notice their light-colored rumps. Nice bull over there, next to the trees. See him?" Libby pointed toward the heavier timber to the east.

"I see him. Where'd you get that scroungy old hat?" Mike asked suddenly.

Libby swept the battered Stetson from her head and examined it carefully. "I've had this hat for many years; I just didn't take it with me when I moved east. Kinda out of place back there, don't you think? Found it a few minutes ago in my old room up at the house. I left a lot of things here when I moved east. Guess I thought I might come back someday. Everything's gone. It's all been trashed out. My old hat was way in the back of my closet on a top shelf. The scavengers missed it. Everything else was stolen or reduced to rubble. Same is about true all through the old house."

"What time did you get up?" Mike asked.

"'Bout four, I guess. Just been looking around."

Libby managed scrambled eggs and some bacon for their breakfast and then, with her coffee cup in hand, headed for the main house again. Structurally it wasn't in as bad shape as she had at first imagined. In her dad's old office she found an ancient telephone book. It was dog eared, and beset by dampness, but its pages were still legible. The phone was there on the counter, but it was as useless as most of the rest of her utilities. Using her cell phone, Libby dialed the power company. She was assured that there would be someone there right away to restore their power. In the old barn Mike found a wheelbarrow, and he and his mother began hauling useless pieces of furniture to their trash pile.

About nine, the utility truck arrived and pulled to a stop by the cabin. Two linemen climbed out of the truck. "You've been disconnected down by the highway several years ago," one of the men stated. "We're going to shut everything off up here before energizing the line. Before you put power on the buildings I'd suggest having an electrician go over everything, make sure it's safe. We'll put power to the meter, but we'll leave the main breakers open."

Libby agreed. "Who's a good electrician to call?" she inquired.

"We've worked with Noberton Electric quite a bit."

"You got a number for them? she asked.

The man consulted a small notebook, scribbled a number on a slip of paper, and passed it to Libby. He then went up to the big house, opened the main breaker and all the others, and removed the meter from its base. He and his partner drove back down the roadway and out of sight into the timber. Libby contacted Noberton Electric and they promised prompt service as a rule of thumb. A few minutes later the utility men were back and did some checking at the main house before plugging in the new meter.

"You gotta sign here," the foreman said, passing a clipboard to Libby. "There's an overdue bill from years ago too. Pretty hefty one at that. You'll have to go by the office and straighten that out. We've got you hot right up to your main breaker panel."

"Thanks, guys. I'll take care of the bill, but probably not till tomorrow."

"No problem there."

The men left and Libby called a glass service outfit, and a floor covering business. This seemingly easy task was complicated by company after company offering to do the work, maybe next week, or the following month. It took several calls, in most instances, before she found businesses that were even willing to try to meet her time frame. Once Libby had to offer a sizable bonus to ensure the work was completed in a timely fashion. They all finally agreed to send out their estimators to assess and measure for what she needed replaced.

A carpenter was called and hired to do any one of a million chores that Libby knew would be popping up everywhere she looked. A few minutes after the utility people left, the sheriff's men arrived and began a detailed examination of the property. They gathered up a few items and finally left, claiming that the place was now drug free. Gordon Taylor wasn't one of the deputies involved in the search.

Libby and Mike continued their morning of trash hauling. In the open expanse of the resort's grounds, Libby gave Mike his first driving lessons. He was very soon able to handle their big pickup as it moved from location to location hauling large pieces of furniture and heaps of trash.

The electrician arrived and step by step checked out the five cabins, the lodge, and the main house. His visit coincided perfectly with the representative of the glass service company. Libby ordered new ceiling fixtures where needed from the electrician's huge catalogue. The glass company representative talked Libby into thermo pane replacements for all the windows in the main house. She then left him to his measuring and note-taking chores and ran off to check on the carpet men. The carpenter arrived and began his day by rehanging the front door on new hinges and changing the lock. Libby was kept quite busy keeping up with everyone.

One by one, the electrician energized the breakers to each of the units. He found little damage, as there had been no power on when the wayward group of people had invaded the resort. Here and there he made a minor repair of a switch or a plug, and he removed all the bare wires hanging from old ceiling fixture boxes. He found nothing major until he returned power to the deep-well pump. The instruments showed that the pump was running, but numerous breaks in the line and many damaged fixtures were preventing any water pressure from building up. Everywhere they looked there were leaks, and the pump was shut off. The electrician left at close to quitting time, and Libby called a local plumbing company.

Libby had a long list of desires. "I know there are at least seven complete toilet units that have to be replaced and probably some of the water heaters too. Piping under the sinks is all broken also. Lord knows how many lines have frozen and need to be replaced. I want it all redone as necessary."

"What's your time frame?" the man asked.

Libby laughed. "I'd like it all done yesterday?"

"From what you've told me, we'll need a little longer than that. I'll send a couple of crews out there first thing in the morning," was the serious response.

It was just beginning to get dark when Libby kindled a small fire in the wood stove and started fixing their supper. She still hadn't called the propane people about filling their huge tank; thus their kitchen range was still inoperative. At least they had lights now, if nothing more, and she was greatly surprised and relieved to find that the refrigerator was apparently working properly. They were just getting ready to eat when they heard the car coming up the hill.

Mike jumped to the window and turned back a moment later. "It's the police again," he announced.

Libby met Gordon Taylor at the open doorway. "Come in, Gordon. You're just in time for supper."

Gordon shook his head. "Thanks, but no thanks. I'm on my way home, done for the day. You got any coffee?" the deputy asked. "I've got time for a cup."

"I didn't have a coffee pot. What there is, is in that pot and it's left over from this morning." Libby pointed to the big pot warming on the back corner of the wood stove.

"I'll try it. You want a cup?" he asked picking up two mugs from the counter.

"Sure. I'll try anything once."

"How's it going?" Gordon asked. He placed their two cups on the table in the center of the small cabin.

"Like you said. It's a mess, but we've started making progress."

The deputy shook his head. "Wow, this is strong," he muttered. He turned to the sink and poised his cup below the spigot and tuned the valve. Nothing happened.

"There's creek water in the jug right there," Libby explained with a grin. "Plumbers will be here tomorrow."

Libby's simple meal of loose fried ground beef, chopped onions, and macaroni filled the small cabin with fragrant odors. Libby watered down her cup of coffee slightly, and she and Mike sat down to eat.

Gordon pulled a chair around to the table. "You need to hire any help out here?" he asked.

"You better believe it," Libby stated. "Lots of help of all kinds."

"What kind mostly."

"Just labor, rub and scrub people, trash haulers and the like. I've already got electricians, plumbers, a carpenter, and a glass company hired."

Gordon pulled a small notebook from his pocket and jotted down several notes. "I'll go by the school in the morning for you. They always have a listing of the teenagers that are looking for work. Most of them will do a pretty good job. How many can you use?"

"Oh, I'd say three or four anyway for probably at least a week. I'd pay them minimum wage."

The deputy slipped his notebook back into his pocket. "I'll see what I can do."

"You said you were going home?" Mike asked.

"Yes."

"But you've got the police car."

"We sergeants keep our cars 24-7. It's like a fringe benefit that they give us. We can use them for our own personal use, within reason, but we're on call 24-7 as well. Works out pretty good for all of us. Even though we're off duty technically, people still see the cars going up and down the road. We're always a working presence."

"Sure you don't want a bite?" Libby asked. "There's plenty to go around."

"No, really. Smells great, but I've got to be getting back home."

"Of course, I'm sorry. I guess your wife will be anxious. It's getting pretty late."

"No wife, but my dog and my horses will be having a fit."

Libby smiled as she glanced at the empty ring finger on the deputy's left hand. "Well you better go and get your chores done," she replied with a laugh.

Gordon rose from the table. "You're right. I've got to get going. Glad all is coming together for you. I'll send you some help in the morning. Have a good night now."

Libby walked the deputy to his cruiser. "Good night, Gordon. Thanks for stopping by. Remember the coffee pot's always on."

Gordon laughed. "That was real old cowboy coffee," he stated. "Would have been better over a campfire."

"I've had a few of them over the years," Libby replied.

"I'll keep that in mind."

The officer was gone a minute later. It had been more than a hectic day, it had been brutal. The utility men had been here, the sheriff's deputies, the glass replacer, the electrician, and the carpenter. On top of that, Mike had had his first driving lesson. The list seemed endless. Libby's feet and legs were very tired and she ached all over more that anywhere in particular. She laid out her old well-worn cowboy boots for tomorrow's footwear, hoping that these boots would be easier on her feet than the jogging shoes she had worn today.

The next day help arrived. Droves of help descended on the resort. Libby and the plumbing company owner toured the buildings and the necessary repairs were set in motion. They began with the deep-well pump and then the main house. Step by step they branched out down the line. The propane company refilled their huge tank and checked all the gas appliances throughout the resort, ensuring that they were all operational and in safe working condition.

By ten o'clock the teenage workforce was on the scene. Mike made several friends almost immediately. Several of the boys arrived driving their own pickups. Libby left the boys alone for a few minutes as they got to know each other. Mike took several of the boys to the barn and showed them his grandfather's old tractor. It seemed to be a common point of interest for all of them.

The day's agenda focused on the main house. The pile of trash and junk was building by the hour. Many of the articles came from the smaller cabins where the intruders had settled. By the end of the day the main house was pretty well cleared of all refuse, and the young group of workers moved over to the communal lodge.

The plumbers, in the course of their duties, had dislocated a family of raccoons that had created a sizable abode in the crawl space under the flooring of the main house. Skipper, Mike, and two of the young hired hands had herded the small band back into the timber where they all quickly took refuge in the tallest of the many trees. Their entranceway to the area beneath the house was boarded up securely. By five o'clock the plumbers and the labor gang had all left, and Mike and Libby were alone again. The onslaught of renovation workers would begin again on Monday morning.

At least they had running water now in the headquarters. Libby had electricity in all the buildings and propane for heating and cooking. She and Mike searched throughout the complex and located the best of the surviving pieces of furniture that they needed. They carried these pieces up to the main house. They began unloading their truck and trailer, storing all of the items in the sturdy log building. To Libby, it was beginning to feel like home once again. Libby and Mike didn't see Gordon Taylor for the entire weekend.

On Sunday morning exterminators paid three visits to "Tanner's Resort" fumigating all the buildings inside and out to permanently rid the premises of all unwanted guests. The exterminator crew stopped their work for a few minutes and helped Libby and Mike slide the big topper off of the bed of their pickup.

Libby and Mike spent most of the time alone scrubbing and cleaning the old house. They finally had suitable bedrooms of their own. The house had a master bedroom on the first floor and two small bedrooms with dormer windows upstairs.

Libby ignored the master bedroom at the back of the house. This would someday become their guest room. She settled down, reclaiming her old bedroom on the second floor. In the late evenings, just as she had done years ago, she could sit quietly on the edge of her bed gazing in silence out across the small valley and the roofs of the guest facilities below her. The dormer window would be open, letting in the fragrant aroma of the mountain world. A gentle breeze would carry to her the crisp alpine chill of the snow fields above the timberline. From where she sat today, Libby half expected to hear her mother's laughter from the shaded front porch below.

She shook her head and reluctantly allowed the reality to settle in. Set aside suddenly were the reflective moments of her life. Her mother's carefree laughter faded to only a memory, her beloved Bill was gone too.

Libby sat a little straighter on the bed as she returned to the present. She remembered her son, so strong, youthful, and determined. His indomitable spirit seemed to rekindle the strength and assurance that had swept over her daily in the past few weeks. Outwardly life was threatening to return to normal despite her subconscious efforts to cling to the deep trauma that had recently affected her.

Mike ignored the spacious main bedroom and chose instead a room in the front corner of the house. This was next to the small office area across from the living room. Years ago this room had been his grandmother's exclusive domain. Here, in the days before the resort, she had spent many private hours with her sewing chores and her needlework while overlooking the daily happenings of the ranch and the rolling meadow dotted with beef cattle and their calves.

On Monday morning the nostalgia was all set aside. Once the workers got going, Libby and Mike took their now empty trailer up to the county seat and turned it in. It was a forty-mile scenic round trip that gave Libby time to just relax. On the way home they bought a huge supply, nearly a full pickup load, of food items to stock their refrigerator and the pantry shelves of the old house.

It took the rest of that week for the plumbers to finish, and on Wednesday the glass company began installing the new windows. On Friday afternoon Libby threw a can of kerosene and a torch into the huge pile of trash and useless furniture. The blaze was spectacular. By near suppertime the fire was nothing but a smoldering bed of coals. Gordon arrived and with Mike stirred the embers with an old rake until nothing remained but ash, glass, and metal objects that at a later date would be shoveled up and buried.

Libby fixed pork chops for the three of them using an old propane barbecue that she located in the barn. They ate on the front porch of the house overlooking the resort and the glowing bed of ashes left over from the fire.

"How far does your property line extend?" Gordon asked sweeping his arm across the expanse of the small valley.

"Up behind the house here, I'd guess probably two hundred yards. Used to be a good fence line across the ridge back there, but it's all gone now. That would be my southern boundary."

Libby pointed back toward the main access road hidden from view by the heavily wooded slopes. "Down there, my west property line is Gomas Creek Road."

"To the north?" She swung her arm in an arc over the roof of the lodge and the row of cabins. "All those trees on the far side of the creek along there are mine. The entire creek's on my land once it leaves the Forest Service domain. North of the creek, behind those trees, is a big piece of grazing land that the folks sold when they went out of the cattle business. That adjoining ranch now belongs to nonresident owners.

"My east boundary is the Forest Service line. It's only about a half mile up the road back there in the timber. Except for this open area here, where the house and the resort are, it's almost all timber country. All in all I've got right at five hundred acres."

"I'm no expert, but from where I stand it looks like you've got some pretty valuable timber resources. You going to log it off?" Gordon asked.

"Heavens no! Too much of our timber is going that way. What I have today I hope to keep as it is. It's beautiful wildlife habitat, a place where people can wander and experience nature at its best. I just love the open areas under those old-growth trees. I think I'll put in a few good park benches out there someday so folks can sit and relax and enjoy the peace and solitude. There's almost no brush at all back in those shadowy forests. I want to share what I have with my guests, with the world. I'll hand it all down someday to Mike and future generations."

Gordon replied quickly, "Good for you, Libby. My feelings exactly." They cleaned up following the meal, watching as true darkness spread carelessly across the mountains. Gordon headed for home and his long-neglected chores, leaving Libby and Mike alone in the small canyon.

The following week new vinyl flooring was installed in all the bath-rooms and kitchen areas where the majority of the water damage had taken place. In a few instances the subflooring had to be replaced as well. The local kids did a great job moving furniture and other items from one unit to another. By the end of June there were two units that were almost completely furnished. Items like the missing mattresses, and other items made of fabric, would have to be replaced at a later date.

Rub and scrub and painting were the prominent duties for the entire month of July. It was hot weather now in Montana, but Libby was accustomed to working in this type of climatic exposure. It hadn't rained for several weeks and the ranchers who were making hay were very pleased. Still this had bred several small forest fires, but none in their immediate area.

She and Mike were in town one evening when they met Gordon Taylor. They had just come from the local hardware store where Libby had bought many kitchen supplies: pots, pans, cutlery, and a thousand other items for the cabins. While unloading a shopping cart into the back of their truck Gordon arrived. He turned on his flashing yellow caution lights, pulled up, and double-parked close beside them. He began placing packages into the truck from their three shopping carts.

"Leave anything in the store for the other customers?" Gordon asked.

Libby laughed. "There are a few areas of slim pickings."

"Heading home?" Gordon inquired.

"Pretty soon," Libby replied.

"How about supper first? It's about that time."

Libby thought for a moment. "Good Lord, look at me. I'm a mess!"

"You look good to me," Gordon replied with a smile.

Libby groaned aloud, as she pulled her Stetson from her dark hair, brushed some dirt from the front of her jeans, and combed her fingers through her ponytail. She twisted around and took a peek at herself in her big passenger's side rearview mirror. With a sigh she relented. "Oh well. I guess it's OK, but let's sit way in the back where folks won't see me."

"Just go on in and find where you'd like to sit," Gordon said. "I'll park my car out back and be there in a minute."

At Dora's Restaurant they had a good feed. During the meal Dora Sanders came from the kitchen and greeted her customers.

"Hi, Libby, Mike. Where did you all find this wayward deputy?"

Libby smiled. "Oh, he just pops out of the woodwork every now and then."

"I don't see much of you lately, Gordy. What's wrong with my cooking?"

"Nothing, Dora, nothing at all. It'd be a forty-mile round trip from headquarters just for lunch."

Dora smiled and patted Gordon on the shoulder. "I know, Gordy. I'm just kidding you."

During the course of their meal two other customers stopped to speak to Libby. One was the retired rancher that Libby's folks had sold a parcel of grazing land to years ago. The other was an attractive middle-aged woman who Libby knew from her school days. It was obvious from the brief conversation that she and Gordon, at one time, had been close friends.

As they were eating their dessert, Gordon came up with an idea. "I'm pretty busy most of this week," he began. "How would it work out if on Saturday I brought my horses up to your place and we all went back into the hills for a short ride?"

"Oh, wow! That would be great!" Mike almost shouted.

Libby raised a protesting hand. "Hold on there just a bit. Let's think this through," she interrupted.

"You need a day off," the deputy declared.

"Please, Mom?"

Libby gave in. "Well, OK. I guess we can spare one day."

Their Saturday outing was fantastic. Gordon arrived as the Emersons were finishing their hearty pancake breakfast. He was driving a big Dodge pickup towing a large four-horse trailer. For the first time they saw him out of uniform. He wore regular jeans and a plaid shirt, but had his service belt and handgun strapped tightly about his waist. His well-worn Stetson and rundown riding boots completed his outfit. Mike watched fascinated as Gordon unloaded the three horses and tied them to the rub-rail along the side of the trailer. The deputy tightened the cinches and from the back of his pickup produced a Winchester carbine. He deftly slid it into the boot on his saddle.

"Is that a real gun?" Mike asked.

"Absolutely!"

"Is it loaded?"

Gordon turned serious. "Every gun you see is loaded, Mike, until you prove otherwise. Don't ever forget that. Can you repeat that back to me?"

"Every gun I see is loaded," Mike replied.

The deputy nodded. "Great! Don't ever forget that!"

Libby arrived a moment later. She was wearing her old cowboy boots as she had almost every day of late. She wore her dirty old Stetson hat as she had ever since she had rescued it from the mountains of trash in the old house. Her jeans and a long sleeved Western-style shirt completed her outfit.

"Take the black, Libby," Gordon said. "Her name's Dixie."

Mike watched in awe as his mother jerked the reins loose from the trailer. She checked the saddle's cinch, whispered something into the horse's ear, and deftly flipped the far rein across the animal's neck. She gathered the reins, turned the stirrup, jabbed her toe into the leather, and with one hand on the saddle horn swung quickly and lightly into the saddle. Libby immediately backed the animal several yards away from the trailer and wheeled the mount about. Mike could tell that she was at home astride the tall animal.

"Here you go, Mike," Gordon announced and freed a big roan gelding from the trailer. He cupped his hands, making a step of sorts for Mike, and boosted him into the saddle. He spent several minutes adjusting the stirrups to the proper length. "Your stirrups feel all right, Libby?" he asked.

"Fine," she replied, shifting her weight experimentally in the saddle.

They were off then. Gordon rode beside Mike, following Libby up the Forest Service road into the timber. He talked horse talk to Mike all the way. At last they picked up the pace. Mike soon found that he was getting the hang of it. They rode for several miles into the low-lying hills spotting several wild creatures along the way. Skipper kept a safe distance from the horse's hooves and trotted happily along the trail.

At one point Mike turned to Gordon and asked, "Do you ever shoot your rifle?"

"Sure. Sometimes, but mostly just to keep in practice. I hunt in the fall too. You ever shoot a gun, Mike?"

"Me? No, never."

"Want to?" Gordon asked.

Mike turned in the saddle and looked at his Mom. Libby gave no sign either yes or no. "Mom?" Mike asked.

"It's up to you, Mike," she replied.

Mike just nodded.

They pulled up and Gordon and Mike dismounted. Gordon walked over to a fallen tree trunk and broke off a six-inch polypore that he carried some distance away. He skewered the mushroom-like fungus on a dead twig jutting out from a tree limb and walked back to his horse. He drew his carbine from the saddle's boot and levered a shell into the chamber.

Gordon pointed down the line. "See that polypore that I just hung up over there?" he asked.

"Yes."

"OK, now, just above it, see that pine cone on that limb?"

Mike nodded.

The deputy quickly raised the rifle and sent a crashing shot through the trees. Their three horses flinched, but didn't spook. The pine cone exploded instantly into a shower of fragments. Skipper let out a yelp of fear, spun on a dime, and raced madly down the trail heading for the safety of home.

"Didn't mean to scare your little dog..."

"He'll be OK," Libby responded.

Gordon shrugged. "OK, son. Now your turn. Let's see if you can pick off that mushroom that I stuck up over there."

Mike took the carbine and levered a shell into the chamber. Gordon began talking the youngster through his sight-picture, breathing, stance, grip, and his trigger squeeze. The weapon blasted a moment later, but the target still hung there.

"I missed," Mike complained.

"Try again. It takes practice."

Mike tried twice more and missed both times. All the while Libby sat in almost a sidesaddle position on her horse with her right knee hooked around the saddle horn. She tightened her reins slightly as the target practice went on.

"Want to try it?" Gordon asked taking the rifle from Mike's hands and offering it to her.

Libby swung her right leg back astride the mare. "Sure," she said. "But it's been awhile." She reached down and took the rifle in hand. She kneed her horse slightly to the right, and with only a second of hesitation snapped the gun to her shoulder and slammed a shot at her target. The polypore disintegrated.

"Gee, Mom!" Mike muttered.

"Not bad," the deputy echoed as he reached up and took his weapon back.

Libby nodded her head once and just smiled.

They finished their ride before sundown and found Skipper sitting silently on the porch awaiting their return. While Gordon and Mike unsaddled and rubbed down the horses, Libby fixed a quick supper for them all. She dearly loved cooking for what she secretly called, her men. Tonight she had corn on the cob, a platter of link sausage, and all the huckleberry pancakes you could eat. These were made with her own sourdough batter and spiced with cinnamon to complement the berries she and Mike had picked right off their own bushes. Standing by the stove, Libby's feet and legs were beginning to ache before the two male diners reached their limits. At this point Gordon took over the cooking chore, and Libby sat and ate her own fill. Following the meal she led Gordon on a quick tour of the resort, showing him all the progress that had been made.

"I think I'll be ready to open up on the first of October. At least for some of the facilities. October and November are the most popular of the hunting seasons. Dad used to be pretty much filled up with hunters every year. Then we have the winter months and the snowmobilers. I hope I can get some of them in here, and I hope it snows a lot. It will help make ends meet."

"Those two cabins that you have fixed up now look really good. Where are you going to get the furniture and all that you need to complete the others?" Gordon inquired.

"A company in Denver specializes in that sort of rustic resort-style furniture. I'm getting together an order right now."

"Putting this all back together must be costing you a bundle. Your resources holding out all right?"

There was a long pause as Libby thought through her answer.

Gordon suddenly shook his head. "I'm sorry, Libby. That was a rotten thing to ask. I withdraw my stupid question."

"Oh, that's all right," Libby chuckled. "I guess lots of folks are wondering about that. I'm doing all right, especially right now. I got the closing papers on my home in Pennsylvania last week. My ledger's still in the black."

"What's that mean, Mom?" Mike asked.

"Means we've still got some money left. In the red means we are broke."

"Well, Libby, I guess I'd better be getting home. It's getting late," Gordon stated.

"Come out for Sunday dinner tomorrow evening," Libby suggested.

"Sorry, but on Sundays I'm booked solid. Have to go up to my Mom's place for her home cooking in the evening."

"No problem. I'll catch up with you some other time."

"I'll see you some time during the week, if I'm not too busy. Everything's looking great around here. Keep at it, Libby. I know you'll get it all just right before too long. Give me a call any time if there's anything I can do for you."

At last they loaded the horses and equipment, and Gordon left a few minutes later. Mike and Libby began washing their supper dishes. Yes, things were taking shape nicely, but it would still be a long time before the resort was functional again and their individual lives were back on track.

CHAPTER IX
Almost Ready
August 3–September 18, 1999

The rest of the month of August was blistering hot. They were not open officially for business; regardless, Libby accepted a phone reservation for a cabin for a full week. She could hardly refuse her sister-in-law Eleanor's request. Naturally there would be no fee charged and the housing for this special guest might be at the main house if they could get the empty guest room furnished in time.

Eleanor arrived at the airport in Missoula where Libby and Mike met her. To the woman from the flatlands of Kansas the trip up the Clamis River valley was breathtaking. She settled into the freshly decorated guest room, and she and Libby had a wonderful time hiking through the tall quiet forests in the immediate area. The Wichita native was spellbound by the grandeur of the towering mountains, deep forests, and rushing streams.

Following their evening meal, on the second night of her visit, Eleanor and Libby were sitting out on the wide front porch enjoying the fresh cool breeze sweeping up the hill from the creek. It had been quiet for several minutes. Eleanor broke the silence in a rather halting manner of speaking.

"Libby? I was talking with my dad a few days ago… Uhh, how's Mike really doing? Dad is awfully worried concerning the boy… He has a long-range plan for Michael and he's asked me to lay it out for your consideration… Dad believes deeply that the boy's welfare is basically at stake. He just…."

Libby interrupted curtly. "Give it to me right from the shoulder, Ellie. What's his plan?"

"Uhh, well… He wants Mike to come back with me, when I return. He'll…"

73

"Enough, Eleanor! This concerns my son obviously." Libby rose from her chair, moved to the open front door, and yelled through the screen door, "Mike! Come out on the porch for a minute!"

Mike appeared a moment later, the screen door banged shut, and Libby escorted him to a chair next to his aunt. Libby backed up against the porch railing, raised one leg comfortably, and sat on the rail. "Now, Ellie, from the shoulder once more."

Eleanor swallowed hard, hesitated, looked first at Mike, and then at Libby. "Mike, your Grandpa Jim wants you to come back and live with him in Wichita. He will put you through a great private academy close to home and provide everything in the world for you just like your dad would have done. He..."

"Forget it, Aunt Eleanor. I'm not interested, in any way," Mike interrupted.

"But, Michael. It's such a great opportunity. You'd grow up with the best of everything." Eleanor turned to Libby. "And, Libby, it wouldn't cost you a red cent."

"That's no issue here," Libby replied.

"I'm not going anywhere," Mike added quickly. "Tell Gramps to come out here and visit us. Me and Mom will show him what the real world is all about."

Mike rose from his chair. "Tell Gramps thank you. I know he means well, but my home is here in the mountains with Mom. I'll never leave."

Mike turned and walked rapidly toward the front door. Libby shrugged, raised her arms, and extended her hands palms upward in a sign of submission. "Thank you, Ellie. And when you get home thank Jim for his generous and kindly offer. I know he has Mike's best interests at heart.... And be sure to extend Mike's invitation for a visit, a prolonged visit even. Jim could come to know the real Michael much better here on his home grounds. Thank you both for loving and caring.... Relax for a minute. I'll go and get us a nice cool beer." The in-depth proposal concerning Mike's future was never mentioned again.

The week off from hard physical work during Eleanor's visit did Libby a world of good. But all too soon the stay was over, and it was back to the days of painting and making repairs of all kinds to the facilities.

They were now on their own, as their young workforce had been let go, and the contractors had all completed their work. Libby's investment portfolio was paying off regularly and they were managing to keep their heads above water.

"What's all that pipe for?" Mike asked late one morning. He was referring to the huge stack of irrigation pipe behind the barn. Almost all of the sprinkler heads had been stolen over the years, but the pipe and its risers were apparently in usable condition.

"When I was a kid we had a big hay field over there across the creek... back of the trees. Mom and Dad sold it when they decided to build the resort. We used to irrigate that field with all those pipes. Changed them morning and night every day. Dad changed the settings in the morning; I moved them after school most every day. I've moved those lines a million times over the years. We had a big meadow here too. Right where the cabins are now."

"We ought to irrigate around here," Mike suggested. "It would be nice and green."

Libby thought for a long moment. "Maybe not such a bad idea, Mike. There was a big main line up above the house by the trees. Years ago Mom watered her garden with it. Let's go see if it's still there."

They hiked up the slope toward the shadowy forest. As they neared the trees they found the pipe and a deep layer of pine needles, leaves, dead grass, and brush. Libby poked and gouged with her boots along the partially buried line searching for the outlets. At last she uncovered one. They followed the line, removing enough of the fallen debris to just uncover two of the big attachment fittings. From a storeroom in the back of the barn Libby found a branch line valve. She installed it on one of the openings and twisted the handle. A big gush of muddy water spewed from the opening, but soon began to slow and then finally all that remained was an insignificant trickle.

They moved slowly up the slope along the line exploring at each forty-foot interval, looking for the next opening. They left the main line buried, but uncovered each of the valves as they came to them. Tracing the main line proper, they soon entered the trees, angling uphill toward the road and the small creek beyond. There were no more attachment valves and they found no apparent damage to the pipe.

At last they reached the creek. The concrete irrigation dam thrusting at an angle out into the stream was still in place, but the heavy steel grating and protective screens were buried deep in many years' accumulations of sticks, logs, leaves, and dirt.

"I had to walk up here every evening. Used to ride my horse sometimes and clean out these screens," Libby advised. "Over by that tree I kept an old spade." She went to the tree, looked about, and just shrugged. The spade was gone.

Mike shook his head. "Boy it's a mess now," he replied.

Libby kicked off her cowboy boots. "Well let's clean it out," she ordered and immediately waded into the cold water.

"You're getting your clothes all wet, Mom," Mike cautioned.

"It's nice and cool—come on, get with it, don't worry, you'll dry." Libby moved deeper, almost waist deep into the chilly fast-moving stream.

Mike joined his mom in the creek and together they began dragging the flotsam and driftwood away from the opening. It took both of them to dislodge several of the larger, heavier pieces. Much of the debris was entwined with other parts of the mini logjam, making it very difficult to pull any one piece free. They stopped now and then to rest and get marginally warm while sitting in a patch of bright sunshine that stabbed through the towering trees. Then it was back to work.

The rushing current swept the dislodged refuse down the stream as they worked. Before long they had the protective screens almost clear. The head gate was in the full open position and water was at last surging into the pipe for the first time in many years.

Libby's teeth were close to chattering and Mike's fingers were almost numb. By now they were both completely drenched. Mike pulled off his wet shirt and tied it around his waist. The hot sun felt good beating down on his bare back. Libby simply wrung out the tails of her shirt, knotted them together across her stomach, and tried to grin and bear it.

They took off back down the line. By the time they reached the open valve, water was blasting from the opening, spraying a huge area of the countryside. They throttled down, closed, and removed the valve and proceeded down the line uncovering and carefully flushing each of the remaining openings. Their main line was at last clear.

By now their clothes had dried almost completely, and the sun was dipping below the mountains. It had been a long afternoon's work, and they hadn't even stopped for lunch. Tomorrow they would pick up a bunch of new sprinkler heads, buy two new tires for their pipe trailer, and connect up a long line of pipe, to begin refreshing their resort's arid landscape. It worked like a charm and in less than a week the whole area was beginning to turn green. They moved the sprinklers every evening after supper, supplying a freshening stream of water to a new area every day. Mike was nearly eleven and was a big strong boy for his age. He quickly learned the art of balancing the long aluminum pipes and soon was having no problem moving the lines by himself if Libby was busy.

Ed Tanner's old tractor sat in the barn with many parts on the engine obviously missing. Its tires had been slashed by vandals. Its front-end loader and backhoe assemblies were nowhere to be seen. Each of the attachments, including the hydraulic lines and controls, had been un-bolted from the tractor's frame and made away with. Libby called in a mechanic. After an hour's examination of the old machine, and several cups of coffee, he turned to Libby, shaking his head dismally.

"I'd suggest buying a good secondhand tractor. In the long run it would be cheaper."

"How about snow removal? Libby asked.

"Concerning your overall equipment needs, I'd suggest getting a regular snowplow blade for that big Ford of yours. Then I'd get a good secondhand backhoe-loader like your dad had. Out here you are always wanting to dig a big hole for some reason, and the front-end loader would be great for removing snow from around the buildings. They have lots of power attachments that you can get too, like posthole diggers and the like. I was up at Anderson's in Missoula last week and they had quite a selection of pretty good-looking units for sale. I'd check them out."

Libby frowned. "That sounds like overkill to me. Why buy a plow for my truck when I can use the tractor? That's all Dad ever had."

"It would just be a lot quicker and a darn sight more comfortable. You could plow the whole place out in jig time. You'd end up with a few places that your bucket loader would be great for getting rid of big snow banks, but for everyday plowing, I'd lean toward a blade on your pickup I'd get one that had the latest hydraulic controls so you could angle the blade right and left as well as just raise and lower it. They also have a switch that the minute you shift into reverse the blade rises, shift back into forward gear and it goes back down. Saves a lot of work and time."

"Could I still use my pickup on the highway?"

"No problem. You could leave the plow attached and still drive to town. On most plows they even have an extra set of headlights mounted up high on the frame. The blade covers up your truck's lights in the grill. And the whole outfit's really quick to disconnect if you won't need it for a while."

In mid-August, Libby went tractor hunting. She and Mike took the full day off and shopped all over the city of Missoula. They did their tractor shopping with a loaner pickup that they were given while their truck was modified by the dealer to handle its new snowplow. Later in the day, after checking several companies, they found one outfit that had everything they desired. They bought a used backhoe/loader tractor, a hydraulic log splitter, a big commercial riding mower, and a good chainsaw. All of these items would be delivered within a week.

Back at the resort that night, Libby disconnected her snowplow parking it in the cover of one of the old sheds. Connecting and disconnecting the heavy blade was not difficult and took only a few minutes. She grimaced openly that evening as she filled in the blanks in her checkbook register. "We can't afford to have many days like this one," she muttered as she closed the computer for the day.

Their tractor and other items were delivered to the resort on Friday, the third of September. The man who delivered the equipment was well versed in its operation and spent over two hours showing them just how everything worked. Just before lunchtime he took his empty flatbed trailer and headed back to Missoula. Libby began playing with their new toys almost at once.

"Let's dig a hole," she suggested.

She pulled on her work gloves and positioned her new rig right beside the big ash pile where they had been burning refuse for weeks. She dropped the bucket and her outriggers, swiveled around in the seat and hesitantly began to dig. It took some time getting used to the controls, but within an hour she had a very deep trench dug in the hard-packed soil. Libby kicked her tractor's outriggers up and used the front-end loader bucket to carefully push the pile of ashes, glass, and nonburnable materials into the trench. Mike worked with a rake, smoothing everything off and gathering up the small pieces that Libby missed. They finally backfilled the deep hole and leveled off the entire area.

"Well, that's that," Libby exclaimed as she shut off the engine and jumped down into the soft dirt. Took me three times as long as it should have," she remarked. "But I'll get the hang of it after a while."

Libby hooked onto the old junk tractor in the barn and dragged it several yards to a small shed that Mike had cleaned out. He wanted to try fixing up his grandfather's old rig.

"I'm sure I can get a book and someday get it running," Mike explained. "We can use it for something around here." Libby secretly doubted the outcome of the venture, but cheerfully went along with the plan anyway.

Mike was back in school now and for the first time in a couple of years seemed to be enjoying the challenge of learning. He never complained about the hard work at home. After school there were usually several things that he helped his mother with, but Libby tried to keep these chores to the minimum. Mike's biggest thrill was mowing the huge area they had been irrigating around the resort. The two rotary mower heads on the John Deere riding mower were set for a high level cut. They didn't want a lawn; they only wanted to keep the green grass in check. Mike watched the mailbox closely and every week or so received a letter from his Grandpa Jim back in Kansas. They were all newsy letters with no mention at all of Mike moving away from Montana.

Their furniture began arriving from Denver around the tenth of the month. All the pieces for the cabins and the lodge were of varied Western designs, while the pieces for the main house were much more traditional. Many of the items in the old house were secondhand, but filled their needs quite well. By now all the windows had been replaced and things around the old house were beginning to appear almost as Libby remembered them.

An old leather couch and chair fitted into the rustic living room nicely as did the end tables, bookcases, lamps, and other items that all had seen better days. A huge wagon wheel chandelier, nearly four feet across, with five oil lamp chimneys on its rim, swung from a heavy rusty chain in the center of the room. The fixture had been electrified to fit the day and age. Libby hung her parents' large wedding picture on the outside wall to the left of the huge wood stove. On the right of the stove she placed a similar-size photo of both of her parents with a corral full of beef cattle in the background.

Libby chose items for her own bedroom that closely resembled the furnishings that she had grown accustomed to as a child. She felt quite at home in the twin-size bed with a bookcase headboard. A recent school picture of Mike and a small portrait of Bill rested on her very old secondhand dresser's marble top. The fact that one corner of the top had a two-inch piece missing didn't seem to bother her at all. It fit well with the large mirror showing definite signs of age.

Libby sat on the edge of her bed holding the five-by-eight candid photo of her mother, taken by her father, so many years ago. She was a beautiful woman, and many people who saw the picture noted a great similarity in Libby's features. This old photo had always been a prize possession and had always been displayed in Libby's bedroom over the years. Libby rose from the bed and crossed to the window where she returned the wood-framed picture to the same rusty nail that had held it during her childhood. Balancing this picture, on the other side of the window was a photo of Mike as a baby.

Two old steel file cabinets, a battered rolltop desk, a tall nondescript bookcase, and a modern computer table served Libby's office well. She had found two antique lamps that stood on the roll top and the customer counter, while a small wagon wheel, four-fixture, chandelier hung in the middle of the room. An eight-by-ten portrait of Bill stood on her desk along with a recent photo of Mike and another of Skipper.

The following weeks were busy as Libby moved furnishings here and there trying to get everything just right. They inventoried each facility, ensuring that there were adequate numbers of blankets, pillows, dinner plates, salt shakers, frying pans, and soup bowls. The list was seemingly endless. Libby thanked God for their computer and its versatile spreadsheets.

A local Realtor, well versed in the mysteries of the Internet world, helped Libby set up her own on-line site for the resort with several links to other advertisers. Flyers were placed in many commercial facilities about town, and they were very soon ready to roll.

On the seventeenth, Libby took Mike to town for a special prime rib dinner. It was his eleventh birthday. Gordon showed up as he had promised, and they had a great evening meal together. As they were leaving the restaurant, Mike noticed a flyer in the window advertising a dance at the Grange Hall.

"Hey, Mom! Let's go to that dance tomorrow night," he proposed.

Libby frowned. "What?" she asked.

"Let's go to the dance. I heard the kids talking about it. They all go."

"How about it, Gordon? Think we should take him to the ball?" Libby asked.

"Guess you could. But I can't make it. I've got to work Saturday night."

"Well, Mike, let's say that I'll try. We'll just see how tomorrow goes."

They spent Saturday morning adding the finishing touches to the main lodge. This building had a communal kitchen and dining area and was well suited for large groups, family get-togethers, and the like. There were a total of six double bedrooms plus the great room with its massive rock fireplace, comfortable lounge facilities, huge oak dining table, and kitchen services.

In the afternoon Libby decided to split some firewood for the lodge and the two cabins that had wood stoves. She and Mike had not used their new log splitter as yet. They towed the small trailer-like unit from the barn, set it up beside the small woodpile, and carefully read the instruction manual. Just where this small pile of firewood had come from was anybody's guess.

Libby finally stepped back. "OK! Crank it up, Mike," she ordered.

Mike pulled the recoil starter and the unit came to life. Libby heaved a chunk of firewood about eighteen inches in diameter into the trough and hit the trigger. The big hydraulic ram shot forward splitting the block in two. Mike picked up one of the halves, placed it in position, stepped clear, and Libby hit the trigger again. After each shot the ram would retract for the next try.

Mike laughed aloud. "Hey, this is easy."

"Easier than when I was a kid," Libby shouted back over the roar of the small engine. "We used an ax, a big maul, and splitting wedges. I'll split; you throw the pieces that are small enough into the truck."

They attacked the woodpile seriously then and soon had a good half load of split wood in the bed of the truck. They shut down the splitter and Mike drove over to the lodge where they unloaded and stacked the supply of firewood in the small woodshed. They quit for the day after this chore was completed.

Mike started washing the supper dishes after supper, and Libby went to take a shower and change clothes. She put on a lightweight, plaid, Western-style shirt and a calf-length, dark blue, denim skirt. She rejoined her son in the kitchen, where she began putting away the dishes that were sitting in the drainer rack on the counter.

"Wow! You look great," Mike exclaimed. "We going to the dance?"

Libby shook her head. "Not with you looking like you do," she stated.

Mike made a dash for the bathroom while Libby settled down at her computer completing her daily entry of events. When Mike returned, his hair was freshly combed and his face was scrubbed clean. His shirt and jeans were his everyday school attire, and he seemed quite comfortable wearing his old jogging shoes. Libby was wearing her old battered cowboy boots with the rundown heels.

They drove to town and joined the exuberant gathering at the Grange Hall. Mike vanished into the crowd of youngsters, and Libby made her way in and out among the crowd. She had a cup of cider from the snack counter and stopped to speak with several people that she recognized. More than once she met old classmates or family friends and was prompted to answer some poignant questions about her past years. It all proved difficult, but she managed. Most of the dancing was being enjoyed by the younger set, while most of the older folks were well satisfied to be onlookers.

Libby didn't know what you called the style; but it was wild, carefree and enjoyable to watch. The small four-piece local band was great and literally filled the small room with its music. Two of the band members she remembered from her high school days. She spotted Mike several times talking with other boys and then caught a glimpse of him dancing, if you could call it that, with a tall, very pretty, young girl of about his age. She wore her dark hair cut short with a few bangs down across her forehead. In some ways, Mike's companion reminded Libby of herself, many years ago. The girl wore jeans and a sweater, nothing designer coordinated, just plain, rugged, everyday attire. The band closed out its current number, and when they started back up it was a waltz tune that swept the room.

Mike was out of place with this new melody. The girl with him took the lead and began talking him through the proper steps. Mike caught on quickly and taking the girl in his arms swung out across the floor. Libby shook her head and smiled openly. Her little boy was coming of age.

"Well, I'll be... Elizabeth Tanner." The voice sounded close by Libby's side.

She turned and looked at the man standing by her elbow. He was vaguely familiar, but stood apart from the rest of the men present. He looked like he had just come from work, wherever that was.

"Let's dance," he invited and, not waiting for a reply, swept Libby into his arms. Out onto the floor they spun. In her mind she kept trying to place this man. Then it came to her.

"Leonard?" she asked hesitantly.

"Didn't recognize me, did you?" The man laughed. "You like my beard?"

"It's been awhile," she said.

Leonard held her close as they moved to the music, way too close. Libby could smell the traces of alcohol on his breath; the fact that he had just come from work without a shower was also quite evident.

"I heared that you was back in town," he began. "You sure surprised me when you took off like that right after graduation. Didn't even say good-bye."

"Leonard, it was a year after I got my diploma, and it had been over for the two of us for almost a year before that. I kept trying to get that through your thick head."

"Hell, Libby. You and me was good fer each other. We had lots in common, had lots of good times."

"Yes, I'll admit there were moments. But then I grew up, you didn't. It just wouldn't have worked out for us, and you know it."

"I've changed now. We…"

Libby interrupted. "Yes, I can tell that. But not necessarily for the better."

"Come on, you don't mean that."

"I'm afraid I do. Thanks for the dance. Right now my feet hurt. I quit!"

The music continued; and Libby tried to pull away, but Leonard held her tightly. They stopped dancing, and Libby struggled politely to get free of his arms.

"Hi, Libby," a voice greeted close at hand.

Libby turned quickly and saw Gordon Taylor standing there with his hand on her partner's shoulder.

"I'm cutting in for a while, friend," Gordon announced politely.

"Oh, no you don't. Not tonight," Leonard snapped back.

"Leonard, let's not push it. I think the lady has had enough right now. Don't you?"

"Keep out of this, Gordon. It's none of your damned business."

Another deputy, close by, moved closer still and placed a burley hand on Leonard's other shoulder. "Leonard, I think you and I had better take a short walk," the deputy muttered in a very low tone of voice that wouldn't carry any further than necessary.

Leonard tried to jerk Libby away, and the deputy dropped his hand to the man's wrist. With a deft motion he slipped a fountain pen between two of the man's fingers. The deputy applied just enough pressure with a one handed, vice-like grip to steer Leonard gently through the crowd toward the door. The pen wedged between the fingers brought painful pressure to bear when the hand was squeezed even slightly. They seemed to be simply holding hands as they passed through the gathering almost unnoticed.

Gordon turned quickly into Libby's arms replacing her previous partner. The waltz continued, and the pair swung easily across the floor. They came close to Mike and his friend, and Gordon waved a quick salute to the young couple as the tune ended. By the snack bar Libby and her partner sipped cider and shared a doughnut.

Libby relaxed. "Thanks, Gordon. I appreciated your intervention out there, believe me."

"I was watching you. Looked like he was starting to give you a rough time. You know him from your school days?"

Libby made a wry face. "Afraid so... See, I have made some bad decisions during my life."

"I guess we have all made mistakes at one time or another. Leonard's not all that he's made himself out to be... I'd give him a wide berth if I were you."

"I certainly will. Thanks so much again."

"I've got to get going. I'm working, remember. My partner, Tony, will have scared the devil out of Leonard by now. You won't have to worry about him anymore tonight. See you next week sometime."

Gordon patted Libby's shoulder in parting and then slowly circled the room, speaking to many people, before leaving by the front door.

CHAPTER X
Open At Last
September 18–November 30, 1999

The remainder of the evening was delightful. The altercation between Libby and her old suitor had gone unnoticed by Mike. He and Libby were quiet as they drove home except for one short moment when they turned onto the gravel surface of the Forest Service road. Here Mike mentioned the darkness.

"Notice how dark it is sometimes?" Mike asked, peering out the truck's side window. "Grandpa Jim likes the dark. He told me all about it in one of his letters."

Libby slowed, stopped, and switched off her lights and the engine. In utter silence they sat for long moments in the darkness. There was no star-studded sky, no moon, no vehicle lights, no ambient glow from a distant city. On the empty Forest Service road they were alone, surrounded by only the true darkness that one would expect to find in the depths of an unexplored cavern or possibly at the very beginning of time.

Libby clicked down her window and studied the sky. "Really cloudy tonight, low overcast blocks out everything. This must be like it was when the world began. I like the dark. Don't you?"

Mike didn't reply, but he secretly nodded in the darkness.

Libby continued. "On clear nights you can see the stars better. Even with no moon, there's still some light." She paused a moment. "Starlight. This is why I don't have any big floodlights at the resort like most places do. I'm like your Grandpa Jim; I love the dark."

They sat for another short while in the stillness, and then Libby started her engine and flooded the scene with the blue-white brilliance of her headlights. They were home in minutes. It was chilly in the old house, and Libby turned up the thermostat just a little on the central heating system's propane furnace. She checked her answering machine and found the tape empty. They each had hot chocolate and then retired for the night.

On Sunday morning they took their pickup about a mile up the Forest Service road. In these heavily wooded areas they found numerous trees that had died over the years and fallen. They made wonderful firewood for the resort. Libby, with her chainsaw, bucked up several of these trunks into twelve-inch lengths; and Mike stacked them carefully in the bed of their truck. It was hard work. The big Ford pickup seemed to be grunting as they backed up the steep road in four-wheel drive low range to get close to yet another tree. As the morning progressed, the sun broke through the dense clouds. It began to warm up rapidly, and they both shed their jackets.

Come mid afternoon they had a huge load, reaching above the top of the cab, and they headed home. By now they were both just about worn out. Libby's clothes were covered with sawdust thrown back by her saw and her shirt grimy and soaked with sweat. Mike was in terrible shape too, obviously showing the hard morning's work that he had just gone through.

They came around a bend in the very narrow roadway and spotted another truck heading up the hill toward them. Libby stopped, pulling as far to the right as she could. The downhill traffic traditionally had the right of way. The other vehicle, she recognized immediately, belonged to the Forest Service. Its light shade of green and its radio antennas were distinctive, let alone the department decal on the truck's door and the "exempt" license plate. The driver didn't try to squeeze by. Instead the ranger stopped directly in front of the loaded truck, climbed out of his cab, and walked up to Libby's window.

"Morning," he greeted glancing quickly at the tired, grimy woman. He then scrutinized her load of firewood with a practiced eye. "Got quite a load there."

"Took us all morning," Libby replied.

The ranger walked to the back of the truck and continued his examination of her load. Libby slipped out of the seat, pulled her dirty Stetson from her head, and using it brushed at the sawdust clinging to her clothes. She walked back to join the ranger.

"Anything wrong?" she asked.

"Don't seem to be anything out of place. It's all dead and down timber as far as I can tell."

"That's always been the law," Libby stated.

"That's true, but you'd be surprised how many people try to bend that law. You know you're probably overloaded. If you get stopped on the highway, they'll undoubtedly give you a ticket."

"No doubt, but I'm not going that far."

"You must be from the resort. I stopped down there, but there was no one around. I heard your chainsaw and thought I'd just do some checking."

"I'm Libby Emerson. I own the lodge. My friends call me Libby. That's my son, Mike, in the truck."

The ranger extended his hand to Libby. "Oh, so you're the young woman I've been hearing so much about. I'm Ted Lewis, district supervisor. First names suit me fine."

Libby pulled off her right hand glove and gripped Lewis' hand. "Pleased to meet you, Ted. Listen, drop by the lodge any time. I usually have a pot of coffee going. If not, I'll make us one."

"I'd like to do that, but not today. I'll back up a ways so you can get by me."

Libby slipped back into her truck. "Thanks," she replied with a smile.

The ranger backed down until he found a wide spot in the road and pulled over. Libby squeaked by and with a wave of thanks headed home. They had just started unloading their wood when the ranger drove by on the road heading for some undisclosed destination. They didn't stack the wood, just threw it into a big pile to be split at some later date. Back at the house, Libby found that her first and most pressing need was to get cleaned up. She felt much better following a shower and a complete change of clothes.

The following week she received three cabin reservations for time periods during the coming hunting season. Immediately following this Libby had two drop-by bow hunters who rented one of the cabins for a week. While Mike was in school, she split and stacked her big pile of firewood. Took her all of two full days.

By the middle of October things were beginning to look promising. Her reservation calendar was starting to get crowded with entries, and they were seldom alone at the resort. For the first time in over four months the balance in her checking account was showing an upward trend. Not much, but these days any increase was welcomed.

Between guests Libby had the house cleaning duties of the various facilities to take care of. This in itself was not too much of a problem. Surprisingly, the guests left the cabins in pretty good shape when they checked out. Of course there were the rare exceptions. Still she had to replenish the linen, make the beds, and do a little tidying up to be ready for the next group. Mike was a big help after school and especially on the weekends.

When Mike was in school there were often pleasant times at the old resort. Ted Lewis dropped in one morning and had coffee with Libby, and Gordon Taylor was a frequent visitor. Before the general hunting season got going he brought his horses up on two occasions, and the three of them went for enjoyable rides in the hills.

It was getting much colder and, following several rainy days, they saw snow on the higher peaks west and north of the lodge. Day after day the snow line lowered, until one morning Mike found nearly six inches of the white powder blanketing the roadway. He guided his mom into position by her snowplow and watched closely as she completed the hook up to her big pickup. He got a free ride down to the school bus stop on the highway. The round trip, down and back, opened up the entire roadway in less than fifteen minutes.

The hunters loved the snow, as it made tracking much easier. Libby recalled vividly her own experiences as a teenager in the hills, and she finally gave in to her fond memories and bought herself a good .270-caliber rifle and a .357-Magnum handgun.

All of the resort property was posted, "NO HUNTING." However, the resort was a gateway to the wide-open Forest Service lands to the north and east. At this time of year, with the hunters all afield, everyone working in the rural environment prudently wore bright blaze orange vests or jackets as their outer layer of clothing whether hunting or not.

One snowy morning Libby plowed the road, got Mike off to school, and glanced at her calendar. There were no changes in clientele scheduled. She changed clothes and dressed warmer than for her routine day. Libby buckled her gun belt holding her Magnum revolver about her trim waist, checked the weapon's cartridges, and picked up her heavy .270-caliber rifle and loaded it. She placed the rifle in the rack across her truck's rear window, unhooked the snowplow from the truck, shifted into four-wheel low range, and headed into the mountains.

She drove slowly, watching the timber and occasional open areas for the telltale signs of deer or elk. The winter wonderland slipped by mile after mile. In several places it was tough going even for the four-wheel drive rig, but Libby managed to get by all the difficult spots. Her truck's all-terrain tires were doing their job admirably. She topped out in an area called Moose Meadows, a sparsely timbered area about six miles from the resort.

She found a place to park where she wouldn't be blocking the road, picked up her rifle, and stepped out into the deep snow. It was almost knee deep here in the higher elevations and the air very cold. Libby draped her long scarf over her battered Stetson, pulled it down snugly over her ears, and wrapped it comfortably about her neck. She hiked slowly, cautiously, ever watchful for sign or sound of her quarry. At last she stopped and hunkered down on her haunches. The rough bark of a stout ponderosa pine was against her back. She remained as motionless as possible as very fine snow began to fall. It was bitter cold, but she remained quite still as the minutes dragged by. The light snowfall didn't obstruct her vision hardly at all. It was almost an hour before a tiny flick of movement caught her eye. Libby turned her head very slowly and spotted the big mule deer buck. He had been resting, rose to his feet, and shook his body head to tail. The range… a bit over one hundred yards.

It seemed like it took forever to bring the rifle from across her knees to her shoulder. She twisted around into a kneeling position ever so slowly, removed her right glove, and thumbed her Stetson and scarf back from her forehead. Libby took a deep breath, exhaled slightly, brought her eye down to her scope, and concentrated on her sight picture. She squeezed the trigger slowly and was almost surprised when the rifle slammed back against her shoulder blasting the still mountain air. The big buck dropped in his tracks, and a stellar jay screamed in alarm as it took flight from the tree limbs high above her head.

Libby rose from her cramped position, stretched her legs, and began moving across the open hundred yards to her kill. Her 180-grain bullet had taken the animal high in the neck, just below his ear. Libby stood her rifle against a tree, uttered a short prayer for her victim, and set about bleeding and field dressing the animal. As in the years past, she was amazed at how hot the deep innards and blood of the animal were on her bare hands. She wrapped the carcass with long lengths of bright orange ribbon hoping that this would deter another hunter from taking a careless shot. Libby tried three times to get the big buck onto her shoulders and the third time ended up flat on her own back in the bloody snow.

Libby uttered a quiet curse at her failure, gave up this idea, slung her rifle across her back, and began dragging the heavy load back toward her truck. The deep layer of snow made sliding the carcass somewhat easier. Still, it was a two-hour trip, but only perhaps a half mile in all. Finally the deer was loaded and she climbed into the cab, started her engine, turned up the heater's setting, and just rested for several minutes as the cab warmed. At last Libby headed back home.

When Mike came in from school, he found a deer carcass hanging in the shed beside the barn its body cavity held open by several sticks to promote cooling. The big mule deer would supply fresh venison for supper and plenty to store in their freezer for special occasions.

"I see Gordon's been by," the boy said pointing to the dead deer.

"What makes you think that?" Libby asked.

"The deer. He brought it to us, right?"

"Nope. That's mine, dropped him back in Moose Meadows about six miles east of here" Libby made her statement trying hard not to change her down-to-earth expression. Mike looked closer at the animal and then at his mother.

"Well I'll be....'" He turned on his heel and, slinging his pack sack of books across his shoulder, headed for the house. "Can I have his horns for my bedroom wall?" he asked, glancing back one time.

"Certainly, when I'm through dressing him out. By the way... They're called antlers."

Mike nodded his thanks and understanding and continued on toward the house.

Libby took a gamble around the first of November. She bought four used snowmobiles and offered them to her guests at a reasonable hourly fee. They were a big hit, and she was strongly considering buying several more. Nevertheless, each of these additions meant that she had more maintenance chores to take care of. There were progressively more items to check out and make sure they were safe and ready for her guests. Libby was quickly becoming an expert in snowmobile maintenance; with the increasing snow depth, she was starting to be quite proficient at snow removal as well. Mike dearly loved the snow machines and spent some of his free time riding them back in the timber along the old logging roads.

In all they were experiencing long hard days and weeks, but the rewards were well worth their efforts. It was nearing the close of the regular deer and elk hunting season, still the calendar showed very few openings in the weeks ahead.

Libby stood in front of the living room window one evening just before sundown. It was snowing lightly and cheerful lights spilled out of several of the cabin windows onto the snow-covered ground. Smoke curled from the chimney of the main lodge and from the two cabins with wood stoves. At different times vehicles came and went. The road was in good shape.

Mike was in his room finishing up an English writing assignment. Libby thought that this obligation had been playing on his mind because for several days he had not really been his old cheerful self. In his spare time of late, he had been working on a new sketch of a clipper ship rounding Cape Horn; this in itself worried her. Most of Mike's sketching was done during times of mental anguish. It was close to bed time when he finally joined his mother looking out over their resort.

Libby turned to her son. "Get your English theme all written?" she asked.

"Yes."

"Want me to review it for you?"

Mike shrugged. "Not really. It's all right."

"Suit yourself." There was a long period of silence. "You all right, Mike?"

"Sure, why?"

"You just seem awfully quiet here of late. Something bugging you?"

Mike didn't reply, and Libby didn't push the subject. The ball was in Mike's court now. They stood together for several minutes watching the darkness as it descended on the small valley.

"Mom? Do you like Gordon?" Mike suddenly asked.

Libby hesitated a moment as she weighed her son's question. "I think Gordon's a very likable person... Yes, I get quite a bit of pleasure from seeing him, from being with him."

Mike thought for a minute. "Last week I saw Gordon at the school. He pulled up with his sheriff's car." There was a long uncomfortable pause.

"Go on, Mike," Libby urged.

Mike swallowed hard. "There was a girl in the car with him, and she kissed him before she got out."

Libby's brows wrinkled, and her frown slowly spread across her entire face. "You mean a girl, or a woman?"

"Oh, just a girl from school."

Libby heaved a quiet sigh of relief. "Probably some friend's child that he was taking to school. Maybe she just missed her bus."

Mike shook his head. "No, Mom. There's more."

"OK, let's have it."

"I know her. She's a third grader. She rides the school bus with me almost every day. I saw her a couple of days ago on the bus; we sat together, and we talked... She says that Gordon is her dad."

Libby felt her stomach muscles tighten. She swallowed hard and tried to put together an adequate response to the startling news. "You're sure you understood her, right?"

"Yes, Mom... I guess Gordon's married."

"Mike, I'm sure there's a good explanation behind all of this. Next time I see Gordon, I'll get it all straightened out. I promise."

Libby spent an uncomfortable night as she dwelled on the surprising news. To begin with, it was shocking for her to find that it mattered at all, that it made a difference to her one way or the other.

The next day she found herself immersed in the operations of the resort and really didn't have much time to think about Gordon. Still, the nagging thoughts in the back of her mind, concerning Gordon's private life and his daughter, wouldn't leave her alone. Two days passed and suddenly one evening his county cruiser swung up the roadway and parked beside the house. Mike was out on the Forest Service road riding a snowmobile at the time, and Libby was left alone with her unpleasant questions.

"Coffee, Gordon?" she asked as he entered the mudroom following a very superficial knock on the back door.

"Love some," he answered. "How've you been?"

"All right, I suppose." Libby poured their cups, and they settled down across from each other at the kitchen table. She cleared her throat noisily and ran her finger around the rim of her cup. "Mike came in with some pretty startling news the other day."

"Oh, like what?"

"Seems like he met your daughter on the bus." Libby looked up quickly to catch Gordon's reaction to her statement.

"Oh, my God," the deputy muttered. He pushed himself away from the table and walked across to the sink. He turned, leaned back against the counter, and looked Libby straight in the eye.

Before he could speak, Libby interrupted. "I've got an idea that this is going to be good," she exclaimed. She could feel the color rising slowly in her cheeks.

"What can I say, Libby?" There was a decided pause. "I've known for a long time that I was in way over my head with you. I wanted to tell you the whole story, but just never seemed to find the right time. I didn't want to ruin the few hours that we enjoyed now and then. I knew it was all bound to come out sooner or later."

"Don't you realize that every minute you spend with me is taking away something from your wife and from your daughter? Our relationship has been completely above board, but still, just being here, like you are now, you're cheating on your poor wife."

Gordon shook his head slowly. "Remember, I told you once that I have no wife, Libby."

"But?"

"I have no wife, Libby! I haven't seen or heard from Charlene in many years. She left Brenda and me five years ago when Brenda was only three. My Mom's been taking care of her ever since. Last I heard Charlene was somewhere in Canada. I finally filed for divorce and it was granted last year."

"And you live with your mother?"

"No. She's way up on Burnt Fork Road. She runs the old family saw-mill out there. My place is down on the highway just outside of town. I usually see Brenda several times a week, but Sunday dinner has always been my big day with Mom and my daughter. Brenda's temperamental and would be livid if I were to miss our regular Sunday time together."

Libby could feel the tension draining slowly from her body. "I'd like to meet your daughter sometime, your mom too. Your dad still living?"

"No, he died back in '68. Mom's got four men working for her, but she's the boss. I've wanted to bring Brenda out here several times, but I didn't quite dare. She tends to get a little standoffish if I'm introduc-ing her to someone I care about. I've never quite known how to handle her at times like this. I've been waiting for just the right time to tell you about my past life and introduce you to my family."

Libby laughed. I know just how Brenda must feel. My dad used to try to introduce me to some of his friends…"

The buzz of a snowmobile cut into their conversation and a moment later a snow-covered boy burst through the back door. He craned his neck to peer momentarily into the kitchen.

"Hi, Gordon," Mike greeted with almost a flat, melancholy tone to his voice.

"Hi, Mike. Cold enough for you?"

"Yes." Mike shed his snow-covered snowmobile suit, hung it on a peg in the mudroom wall, and joined the adults in the kitchen.

Libby pushed a chair out from the table with her toe. "Mike, Gordon's bringing his daughter out for supper pretty soon. I'll want you to intro-duce her to me." Libby made her statement in a very matter-of-fact way. "Maybe she can just get off the bus with you. Gordon can come when he gets off of work and we'll all eat together."

Mike paused in the act of seating himself. "Mom?"

"I'm not married, Mike," the deputy advised. "My wife vanished many years ago. Yes. Brenda's my daughter, and I hope you and she will always be good friends."

Mike eased himself down into his chair. "Oh, wow! I thought…" The grin on his face was worth a million apologies.

Libby laughed. Gordon returned to the table, and the three of them began talking of the winter season and what it probably held in store for them. It was amazing how quickly the subject and the atmosphere could change. Libby was forced to break away for two phone calls and then busied herself fixing their evening meal.

Gordon headed home following the meal and Mike dove into the small amount of homework that was due tomorrow. Just before bedtime Libby stopped by Mike's room to say good night. She found him deeply engrossed in sketching a clipper ship, this one tied securely to a busy wharf. In the background, in place of the usual rolling storm clouds and lightning, Libby saw a beautiful sunset. For Mike, it was an obvious change of setting; it made Libby smile.

CHAPTER XI
Holiday Time
December 1–December 31, 1999

With November fast coming to a close they had a completely different clientele. Gone for this year were the hunters. Their guests now were the snowmobilers, photographers, cross-country skiers, and snowshoers. There were always a few who just wanted to sit by the fire and enjoy the solitude of their rustic cabins.

Such was the case for Eric Applebetz when he arrived unannounced just after Thanksgiving. He refused the free guestroom accommodations, preferring to spend much of his time alone in one of the cabins with a whispering fire in the wood stove for company. On occasions he could be seen standing in the snow on the bank of the creek quietly watching as the water in the stream flowed endlessly toward the Pacific where it would begin its eternal cycle anew. At these tranquil and reflective moments, Skipper often joined the quiet man and sat motionless in the snow by his side. Perhaps they communicated. From a distance it was hard to tell. The lawyer had found a spot where he could set aside the constant turmoil cluttering his mind every day of his hectic life. He and Libby spent many hours in her comfortably appointed living room discussing legal, investment, and financial matters and strategies. Following his unique stay, Eric returned to Philadelphia. He left a reservation for the following year on the same dates. Next year he hoped his wife would accompany him to his newfound paradise in the mountains.

One day in early December Gordon called on the phone just after breakfast. "Hi, Libby. Anything special on your agenda this evening?" he asked.

"Not that I know of. Why?"

"Thought I'd drop by for supper. I'll bring some seafood for the meal, if that's all right. One of the county judges had a bunch of fresh seafood flown in from the coast for a party, and he's found that he has quite a surplus."

99

Libby smiled. "Sounds good to me."

"OK if I have Brenda walk up with Mike from the bus? You'd have to look after her for probably two hours before I can get there."

"I'd love to have her. No problem at all."

They ended their call, and Mike was brought up to date on the plans for the evening as he finished his breakfast. He did not seem overly thrilled by the prospects, but accepted the responsibility of being Brenda's host without undue comment.

Winter was setting in with a vengeance. It started snowing just after breakfast time and poured it down all day. It wasn't too cold. The thermometer hovered around the twenty-degree mark and the wind blew at a steady ten miles per hour. Libby cleaned house a little more than she normally did. She wanted to make a good impression on her special guest.

Libby had become quite adept at handling her plow-mounted truck and her tractor. She enjoyed the challenge of plowing and removing the snow from the road and parking areas. About noontime she took the truck out and bladed the road down to the highway. She scraped and piled the snow high all around the parking areas by the cabins. At some places along the road she was able to push and dump the snow into the running waters of the creek. Libby loved to watch the surging current as it quickly washed the snow away carrying it downstream away from the resort. The four guests they had were doing well and enjoying everything. Libby hauled some firewood down to the two cabins using wood stoves. In all it was a very busy day.

Late in the afternoon, just before time for the bus, she made another run with her rig down to the highway. She thought about meeting the bus and giving the kids a ride home, but decided against it. The scenic and private walk through the snowy countryside would be good for both of them following a long day in school.

Just after three Libby sat at her desk and watched from her office window as the twosome plodded up the hill through the falling snow. In the kitchen she turned the burner on beneath the teakettle and prepared the makings for two cups of hot chocolate. Just as the whistle on the kettle began to scream, the back door opened and Mike led the young girl into the mudroom. The pair stomped the snow from their heavy boots.

"Hi, Mom. We're home," Mike called.

"Hi yourself," Libby answered. She poured the boiling water into the two cups, turned, and entered the mudroom.

Mike and his friend turned to greet her. "Mom, this is Brenda Taylor. She's Gordon's daughter."

"Welcome to the wilderness, Brenda. I'm certainly glad to meet you. I've heard a lot about you from your dad."

"Hi, Mrs. Emerson. I live in a wilderness too. It's just a house, a sawmill, and some old barns and sheds. But I've got my own horse to ride."

"By the way, just call me Libby, all right? Here, give me your foot."

Libby bent to one knee as Brenda dropped onto a bench. One by one Libby helped the girl remove her cumbersome winter boots. Mike and Brenda hung their coats and hats on the numerous heavy pegs in the wall and followed Libby back into the kitchen.

Here! Careful, this stuff's hot!" Libby warned as she handed the cups of chocolate to the youngsters. "When I grew up here, Brenda, I had my own horse too. They are a lot of fun."

From a cabinet Libby produced a bag of marshmallows and placed them on the table for the kid's enjoyment. They talked while they sipped their chocolate. When the cups were empty Mike turned to his mother.

"Can I take Brenda for a ride on one of the snowmobiles?" he asked.

Libby slowly shook her head. "Oh, I don't know about that," she began. "I think you'd better wait and check with Gordon."

"Oh, my dad lets me ride. We've got one out at Grandma's, but I have to stay right close to the house."

"Well, all right. Just for a while. Stay right here around the house, and no rough horseplay, OK?"

"We'll be careful," Mike promised.

The youngsters bundled up and a few minutes later Libby watched from the window as they drove back and forth around the resort. It was getting darker by the moment. The snowmobile's lights were always on so the scene was brightly illuminated ahead of them. They were just turning back toward the buildings on the old road when Gordon came into sight. He flipped on his bright red and blue warning lights and gave the kids a quick blast of his siren. Mike stopped abruptly as the prowl car moved by. They all waved to each other in passing, and Mike chased the car up the hill to the house.

Gordon had brought a variety of seafood for their supper. It was quite enough to feed at least ten people. Libby started putting together a big tossed salad and a rice dish to go with their meal, and Gordon rolled up his sleeves and began cooking the several types of seafood. The main course would be halibut steaks with side dishes of steamed clams and oysters on the half-shell. These latter items proved to be a real challenge. Gordon spent several minutes with Libby's cookbook before he found out what to do with the oysters and the clams. Libby searched her pantry and located two cans of spinach which would go well with the steamed oysters.

While the adults were busy in the kitchen Mike took Brenda to his room and showed her his collection of clipper ship drawings that he had made. She acted vaguely interested, but was much more excited by his collection of CD recordings. This fascination with Mike's musical library turned quickly to disdain when she found only country-western and a complete void in the modern rock music field.

It was soon time to eat. They all gathered about the table where Gordon had just set down a large bowl of steamed clams and a platter of half shelled oysters as their appetizers.

"I don't like seafood," Brenda said quietly.

"What would you prefer?" Libby asked.

"Pizza!" was the quick reply.

Gordon turned quickly from the stove. "It's seafood tonight. Try it. You'll enjoy it."

Brenda ducked her head at her dad's words and sheepishly tasted one clam, and then several more dipped in drawn butter. The youngsters dared each other to try the oysters. Brenda smiled after swallowing, while Mike grabbed for his water glass. At first Brenda shunned the spinach side dish, but soon learned that it was a very complementary companion to the savory oysters. Libby located a bottle of bubbly apple cider, which she served to the two youngsters in tall goblets. She and

Gordon shared a bottle of Chardonnay. This wine was especially well suited to their seafood dinner. They all lingered over their meal and eventually ate their fill. Libby served ice cream for dessert.

At just past seven they called it quits for the evening. Tomorrow was a school day and Gordon had to take Brenda out to her grandmother's house before he went back to town. Mike helped with the cleanup chores following their big meal. After this meeting Brenda became a frequent guest, especially when Gordon visited for a meal.

Now and then Gordon and Libby met during the day for a few private moments. On one such day Gordon found Libby to be quite out of sorts for some unknown reason. She was just not her old cheerful self.

"You feeling bad?" he finally asked pointedly.

There was a long pause as Libby leaned against a kitchen counter playing with her cup of coffee. They made eye contact a moment later and Gordon spotted a warning sign deep in her beautiful brown eyes. It was just that intangible flicker in the depths that law enforcement officers were always watching for. The danger sign was at times the hint of something hidden deep below the surface. He moved forward with caution.

They finally settled down together at the kitchen table, and Gordon began tactfully probing a little deeper. "Libby? You and Mike at odds about something?" he asked haltingly.

"Me and Mike? Goodness no. We're doing just fine."

"Well something's bothering you. I've been here for almost a half hour and you haven't said three words."

Libby looked quickly away. "I'm sorry. It's just a bad day for me." She paused twisting away from the table in her chair. Libby rested her left elbow on the hard surface and propped her head up with her fist. "Today is my anniversary... Bill and I would have been married for eleven years if he hadn't died..." She cleared her throat quietly as her voice almost broke.

Gordon rose from his seat, circled the table, and stopped close behind Libby's chair. He placed his hands quietly on her strong shoulders for a long silent moment. Libby raised one hand placing it over his and squeezed his fingers slightly.

"I can't believe that I'm still grieving," she whispered. "It's depressing at times, but then I manage to push the memories away and I'm all right again. I'm sorry, Gordon. On some days I'm just not myself."

"I understand," Gordon replied.

Libby rose from her seat, turned slightly to face her visitor, and then stepped forward into his arms. She buried her face on his shoulder. Libby cried silently for several minutes as he stroked and caressed her back and the long shimmering strands of her dark ponytail. Suddenly she jumped and pushed herself away.

Libby tried to back across the kitchen. "I'm sorry, Gordon. Please, I'm really all right."

Gordon didn't allow her to retreat completely. He held her at arm's length for several seconds and then leaned forward and kissed each of her tear stained cheeks. At last in parting he placed one lingering kiss on her soft lips. "I've got to be going, Libby," he stated.

Libby jerked a paper towel from the dispenser above her counter, wiped away the salt tears from her cheeks, and blew her nose noisily. "Thanks for dropping by... I'll be all right now. Just seeing you for these few minutes will make my day easier. I'll be all right now."

The deputy picked up his hat and left the house. Libby stood in the cold doorway for a long minute watching as he drove down the long driveway past the cabins. As his car vanished into the trees she turned back to the house and her regular routine.

That evening Libby and Mike took a snowmobile into the woods, and for the first time in Mike's life they cut their own Christmas tree. In the days ahead the house was decorated with a string of colored lights following the contour of the roof. In each window appeared a single illuminated candle. On the front door they hung a holiday wreath that Libby and Mike created with pine boughs, other natural offerings from the woods, and bright red ribbons. Their tree was adorned with countless heirloom ornaments showing that the Christmas season was well on its way. It was a picture-perfect setting as Mike and Libby stopped on the lower road one evening and surveyed their domain. Smoke drifted in a thin white plume straight into the bright sky from the ancient wood stove in the main house.

Gordon and his daughter would drop by in the afternoon on Christmas Eve, but on Christmas Day he would be with his mother for a home-style dinner and all the festivities. Libby and Mike were invited, but respectfully declined the invitation. With guests at the resort and occasional reservation activity, it seemed prudent to stay at home. It turned out that over the holiday they only had one guest and that was a five-day booking beginning three days before Christmas. But the reservation calendar looked promising again following New Year's.

Libby and Mike had just finished eating on Christmas Eve and were getting ready to watch a video movie called, *Christmas Wife*. Suddenly a car drove up to the house. Libby answered the door and found Ted Lewis standing there in the cold. Beside him was a tall, handsome woman.

Libby smiled. "Hi, Ted. Come on in, both of you."

"Merry Christmas, Libby," the ranger greeted. "This is my wife, Wilma, but everyone calls her Willy. Just thought we'd drop by for a few minutes to say hello."

"Oh, I'm so glad that you did."

Wilma nodded. "I guess it gets pretty lonely way out here, doesn't it?"

Libby paused. "It is quiet, but we enjoy it most of the time. Here, let me take your coats." Libby took their wraps and handed them to Mike. "What would you like to drink?" she asked.

"Just anything that's warm," Wilma replied. She turned to study the ornaments on Libby's Christmas tree. "Very beautiful… Some of these decorations are very old, I can tell."

"A lot of them were from my husband's family."

Ted and Wilma backed up to the big wood stove, savoring its warmth.

"Your parents?" Wilma asked, nodding toward the pictures flanking the stove.

"Yes."

"My, but you have done so much around here in such a short time," Willy observed looking around at the simple yet comfortable living area.

"We've been quite busy since we arrived," Libby replied.

"Ted drove me by here over a year ago. It was in pretty bad shape back then."

"Things are changing now."

They had coffee a few minutes later and Libby brought out some fruitcake and Christmas cookies to tempt her guests. They spent over an hour with easy holiday conversation. The wood stove on the far side of the living room crackled merrily, and the decorations on the tree, and at other places about the room, danced and quivered as the radiant waves of heat from the stove drifted past. Eventually the visit came to an end; the Lewis's left just before eight. After the pleasant interval, Libby and Mike went back to their original plan and watched their chosen movie.

Later that night Libby cried for the second time in many months. It was Christmas Eve, and she suddenly missed her husband more than she could imagine. At first it was a sleepless night and then simply a restless one.

The first thing in the morning Libby cranked up her truck and plowed the road and those areas of the resort that needed to be kept open. Mike had breakfast already started when she returned to the house just before daylight. There was no mention of Bill during the day, yet they both sensed the closeness of an invisible being in their lives. They were plagued by an unseen presence that cast a shadow of remorse over the seemingly festive occasion.

Christmas day was laced with nostalgic memories which both Libby and Mike tried to discreetly set aside. This holiday they were alone and were making the best of it. Gordon spent the day with his mom and daughter, but called on the phone, shortly before noon, and talked with each of them for several minutes.

The resort had only one cabin rented over the holiday, and in the middle of the afternoon Libby and Mike walked down and spent an enjoyable hour talking and celebrating with their guests. The older couple was from Florida and they were thoroughly enjoying the Christmas season in the snow-clogged mountains of Montana. Libby invited her guests to share Christmas dinner with them, but they respectfully backed away from the offer. They already had a small turkey roasting for their own traditional feast.

Libby and Mike ate their Christmas dinner just before dark. It was a somber meal, as Bill's absence was greatly felt at the festive holiday occasion. Still nothing was openly said about this by either of them during the meal.

Mike pitched in and began the dishwashing chore while Libby busied herself putting away the many leftovers from their feast. Mike turned from the sink suddenly and in a very quiet voice said, "I miss Dad so much some times."

It was silent for a long moment. Libby turned from the table to face her son and then moved quickly across the room. Tears welled up in her dark eyes, as she gathered her son into her arms. They held each other close for a long time while neither of them spoke. Their grief was difficult to silently control, but somehow they both managed.

Libby finally pulled away. With a chuckle she reached back and tugged gently at the wet back of her blouse. "Your hands are all soapy and wet," she exclaimed.

"Sorry, Mom," Mike replied drying his damp hands on his jeans.

Libby smiled and went back to wrapping the ham for storage in the refrigerator. Following the cleanup chores they both withdrew to the living room. They tried the TV for a few minutes, but found nothing of particular interest. They both retired to their private areas. Mike to his room and Libby to her office where she quietly surfed the Internet.

During this interval she twice had a "New Mail" announcement pop onto her screen. She spent some time on the phone as she completed the business end of leasing out one section of the lodge and the number four cabin. Each of the leases was for a week. Libby finally took a break.

She glanced in at Mike's open bedroom door before going to the kitchen to get herself a snack. He was busy at his small desk sketching. Even from a distance Libby could tell it was another clipper ship, obviously weathering a dark, stormy sea. She frowned. Mike had always sketched only storm-wracked scenes when he was bothered by current events. His mastery of angry cloud and wave had always set the stage for his detailed ships of sail. More recently they were done when he was plagued by thoughts of that one terrible day when his father had died. Mike's silent grief seemed to direct his talents back to the sketchpad. Libby was puzzled by his outward form of expression, but she felt that the intensity of his heartache would someday probably pass. For now she was glad that he had found a manner with which he could express his grief.

At close to bedtime Libby went back to the kitchen and fixed herself a gin and tonic nightcap. She turned to the hallway and called to Mike. "Come in the kitchen, Mike." Libby got a can of 7-Up from the refrigerator as the boy arrived.

Mike didn't say a word as his mother began pouring. She passed his drink to him and raised her own in salute.

"Hope you had a Merry Christmas, Mike. Hope you have many more down the road."

"You put anything in it?" Mike asked.

"Nope. A few more years and then we'll see."

Mike raised his glass. "OK... Thanks, Mom. I know we're going to do all right alone. Aren't we?"

"We sure are."

They chatted and sipped their drinks for several minutes and then Libby called it a night. "I'm going to bed, Mike. Don't forget to let Skipper out for a minute before you turn in."

"You let him out, Mom. I'll bring him back in before I go to bed."

Libby rose from the table. "OK!" Then she called out, "Skipper, come," and the little sheltie appeared as if from nowhere. Libby opened the back door and the little dog dashed out into the snowy night.

Libby halted briefly with the cold night air drifting into the room through the open door. She smelled the faint traces of wood smoke from the cabin down below and the sweet, fresh aroma of the surrounding timber hidden by the cloak of the winter night. It was really cold. Glancing up she saw a few stars here and there. It was partly overcast, but it wasn't supposed to snow, not tonight. Libby closed the door and turned to the living room. She added two large chunks of firewood to the big cast-iron stove, turned the dampers down to the low-fire position, and paused for a moment to absorb some of the welcomed heat. Then she stretched sleepily as she walked slowly down the long hallway. Passing the archway into the kitchen she paused, yawned, and spoke to her son.

Libby groaned. "Night, Mike. Don't forget Skipper." She turned toward the stairway leading to her second-floor bedroom.

CHAPTER XII
The New Year
January 1– January 19, 2000

January swept into the valley with storm after storm. Snow fell almost endlessly. If it wasn't snowing it was blowing and drifting. Libby was glad that she had invested in the big blade for her truck. Unless going to town, she had all four wheels of her rig chained up for the best traction possible. Most of the time she carried a level load of firewood in the bed of her truck for additional weight. She had a flashing amber strobe light attached to the roof of her rig and an additional pair of high intensity headlights mounted on the roof. With the existing lights on the plow frame the four lights gave her plenty of visibility in the black of night. In the blowing snow, even at high noon, these extra lights occasionally seemed quite futile. At times it was a winter whirlwind complete with white-out conditions and all.

Libby found quickly that she enjoyed plowing snow. Her plow controls were mounted on a small clipboard type platform that attached quickly with a spring-steel band to her right thigh. The up-down, right-left angle, and blade tilt switches were always right at her fingertips. Just off the edge of the road she and Mike had installed tall stakes with bright red tops marking all the places where troublesome rocks protruded from the roadway. At these stakes Libby would slow to a crawl as the heavy blade scraped up and over these obstructions.

Depending on the terrain the blade would be angled to the right or the left, throwing a huge plume of snow off its curved blade. In some areas the rolling mountain of snow would be thrown directly into the creek where the rushing water would carry it away.

In other places the blade would be set almost straight and Libby would push the white accumulations, one pass after another, into huge piles. This was particularly true around the parking areas of the cabins. Here Libby would push the deep snow into towering piles. During these forward and back maneuvers the blade would automatically rise from the roadway every time she stopped and shifted to reverse. Shifting back into forward gear would drop the plow back into its working position.

These big piles of snow usually became the property of Mike after school. Their tractor with the large front-end loader was just the tool for removing these deposits and dumping them into the swiftly flowing waters of the creek. The young boy, soon to become a man, had learned the tractor's operation well.

Their guests came and went, many arriving after hearing about the resort from previous customers. Libby and Mike were doing well in all respects, but with their success came hours of just plain hard work. As the guests checked out, Libby went to work readying the unit for the next occupants. She learned quickly to give herself a day of open booking between one guest and the next. Sometimes it was just very hard to find the hours needed where she could go to town for supplies and other business.

The drifting snow created perfect conditions for the winter sports enthusiasts, but it also put a strain on time required for snow removal. At times the road had to be cleared three or four times during the day. They had a small, self-propelled snow blower that they used to keep the entryways open to the cabins and the house. When push came to shove there was still the old-fashioned snow shovel that seemed to be in constant use every day.

Between cleaning cabins, catering to her guests' needs, and replenishing firewood supplies at the house, lodge, and two cabins, there was little time left for the equipment maintenance. Many days, or more appropriately nights, would find Libby refueling snowmobiles, making mechanical adjustments to the machines, or plowing the road just one more time before she crawled into her bed. It seemed as though she was hard at it, 24-7, and she loved every minute of it.

Of course there were other times, the unmentionable moments when everything seemed to go wrong. Like the day she backed her truck into a ditch and had to walk over a mile to get the tractor to haul it out. Then there was the Sunday morning when the septic tank quit working with no pump-out services available until Wednesday morning at the earliest. And the day she slipped and sprained her ankle just walking out to the barn. The injury took over a week to mend, forcing Libby to move about on crutches for the duration. For that week she hired a helper full time and it worked out well.

Mike in the meantime was busy at school, but usually anxious to get back to the resort and back to work. By now he was well trained and quite competent at the use of the big tractor in the snow removal chores and was learning rapidly the idiosyncrasies of the snowmobiles. Along with his art talent, he was a good student, and was learning quickly the use of hand tools. Besides working on the snow machines he spent a few leisure hours each week working on his grandfather's old tractor. Libby allowed a nominal cash flow from her son's bank account for this project, and she was surprised at how far Mike was able to stretch each precious dollar. His needs were made known among his friends, and occasionally he would return home from school with some old, nondescript tractor part poking out of his backpack. He was also becoming a pretty decent cook. Many times he fixed supper for the two of them while his mom was still tied up with other chores.

Gordon and Brenda were frequent visitors and Gordon always pitched in with the numerous tasks that needed attending to. One unusual day Brenda worked for over an hour in the bitter cold shed helping Mike install something on the ancient tractor. Most of the time, however, Brenda wrapped herself snug in the corner of the living room working on some school project or browsing through her copy of *Black Beauty*.

Several times Gordon and Libby found two snowmobiles available, one for the kids and one for themselves, and they were able to take to the hills for short scenic outings on their own. They often played hide and seek among the old-growth stands of timber. Usually Mike and Brenda would take their machine and scamper off on a side trail leaving the two adults alone. For a few minutes of their fast-paced lives Libby and Gordon could be by themselves, and they could throw themselves into all of the preliminaries that romantically inclined beings have yielded to for centuries past. But all too soon the hands of the clock would signal an end to their private time, and they would have to head back to the resort.

One day in mid-January, Libby was faced with one empty cabin for the night, no blizzard sweeping their countryside, and plenty of time to fix a good supper. She turned from the stove, greeting Mike as he came in from refueling several snowmobiles. "Hi, Mike. All done?"

Mike went to the sink and began washing up. "Yeah, for now, I guess...By the way. Have you seen Skipper?"

Libby thought for a minute. "Well, he was chasing around after me all morning; but, come to think of it, no, I haven't seen him in quite a while."

"I just happened to think. I haven't seen him at all since I came in from school. Most of the time he meets me at the bus."

"You call for him?" Libby asked.

"Yes."

"Oh, I wouldn't worry. He won't want to miss his supper. He'll be back before long. He's probably out there just chasing some quail or a cottontail. You know him."

But Skipper did miss his supper. By dark that night the little sheltie had not returned home. Mike checked with all the guests, but no one had seen him. Libby and Mike took snowmobiles and searched the Forest Service road and several other pathways, stopping and calling, listening for his bark, and looking for fresh tracks. By bedtime they had not turned up a single clue as to Skipper's whereabouts.

Mike reluctantly went to school the following day leaving his mom to do the chores and hunt for their small companion. By nightfall of day two he was still missing. By the end of the week there had been no sign of him. At a solemn conference at the dinner table it was finally agreed that their little friend had gone where all little dogs go, across the Rainbow Bridge. Skipper was constantly on their minds. He would always be missed; he would always be remembered.

Two busy days slid by, and tonight's supper was already simmering on the stove. Libby sat at her desk in the office answering an e-mail from Eleanor on her computer. She glanced over her shoulder from time to time watching for Mike to come up the road from school. She clicked the send button as she finally spotted him. A smile and a nod of recognition flashed across her face. Yet something was wrong. He was carrying his coat in his arms, and Libby could not see his backpack of school supplies. She frowned at his almost staggering steps. A surge of anxiety flashed through her body and she dashed to the front door.

Something was definitely wrong. Libby raced down the snowy slope toward her son. The fifteen-degree air knifed through her thin blouse chilling her to the bone as she ran down the slippery hillside. As she closed the distance she noted that his clothes were glistening wet, cold, and clinging to his body, and his warm hat was missing.

"Mike!" she yelled.

Mike staggered and almost fell. She reached him a moment later and grabbed him about his wet shoulders. He only gasped in recognition. Libby grabbed at his wet coat, clutched so closely in his arms, with the intent of placing it about his shoulders. Mike guarded the coat tightly; with gasping breath, and chattering teeth, he blurted out two words, "It's Skipper."

Libby jerked the nearly frozen coat flap aside and saw the lifeless, wet, mangled, tawny and white fur of the small dog. She literally ran toward the house dragging Mike along. Tears were pouring down her face by the time she dragged the stricken boy into the warm room. She led him into the bathroom, turned on the shower, and while waiting for the hot water to arrive thrust him into the stream. Mike gasped as the cool water struck him. Libby adjusted the temperature and gingerly took the coat containing Skipper's remains from his arms. She placed the bundle in the bottom of the tub and began rubbing Mike down. He finally stopped shivering, some color began to reappear in his face, and he began turning round and round beneath the warm spray. Libby heaved a big sigh of relief and began removing his outer garments. She noted for the first time several places where he had some pretty deep abrasions on his hands and arms.

The sleeves and front of Libby's shirt had become soaked as she worked on her son. "Where was he?" she asked.

Mike shivered slightly. "In the water on the other side of the creek. He was caught on a snag just under the edge of a heavy ice and snow shelf. I just happened to see him."

"You should have come and got me to help. You could have..."

"He could have been washed away, Mom."

"OK. You did what you had to do. It's all over now. You stay in here and get good and warm. I'll take Skipper and put him in the kitchen sink for now. We'll bury him later."

"I'm sorry, Mom."

Libby turned toward the bundle in the bottom of the tub. "It's all right, Mike. These things just happen sometimes."

Libby gathered up the little dog still wrapped in the drenched coat and quickly carried it dripping to the kitchen. She placed it in the sink and went upstairs where she changed her wet blouse. She returned to the kitchen and had just finished wrapping Skipper's remains in his little blanket when Mike arrived covered only by a towel.

"You go get dressed," Libby ordered.

Mike looked at his mother. "How are we going to bury him?"

"We'll have to keep him in the big freezer till it gets warmer and the ground isn't frozen so hard."

"Oh, Mom?"

"He's already frozen, Mike," Libby replied. "He'll be glad we're taking good care of him... You go get dressed. I'll take care of Skipper."

"No, Mom. We've got to bury him. Use your backhoe. It'll break through the frozen ground."

Libby thought through the problem, and finally agreed. OK, Mike. After supper we'll see what we can do."

They parted and several minutes later met at the kitchen table where Libby treated Mike's few injuries.

"Where's Skipper? the boy asked.

"On the back porch where it's cold."

Libby fixed her son a cup of hot chocolate. He was drinking this when someone knocked on the door. Libby answered and recognized one of her guests.

"I just came back from town and found this packsack down by the side of the road near the creek. I think it's probably your son's. Did he lose it down there?"

"Yes, thanks so much. He fell in the creek, but he's all right. Thanks for bringing it up here." The woman left a moment later and Libby went back to the preparation of her evening meal that had been interrupted by the emergency.

It was very quiet during the meal. Libby never thought of Bill's death the anniversary of which was upcoming tomorrow. She was just too overcome with thanks that her son was all right, and a sad chapter in their lives was at last coming to a close with the finding of Skipper's remains. Following the meal they both ignored the supper dishes, turned instead to the mudroom, and began slipping into their warm winter coats and boots. Neither said a word.

It was dark on the small back porch. Mike stopped by the blue and white plaid blanket that held his small friend.

"Get a flashlight, Mike. I'll get the tractor. We'll carry Skipper in the bucket while you find a good place for him."

"No, Mom! I'll carry him."

"All right… I'll get the tractor. Go ahead and find where you'd like to bury him. I'll be right along."

Mike nodded agreement, turned back to the house for a flashlight, and paused uncertainly again on the porch. The body of his friend was at his feet. He slipped the light into the hip pocket of his jeans and bent down to retrieve the still, blanket-wrapped, form. He was surprised at how heavy Skipper was.

From the barn Mike heard the roar of the tractor as Libby started it. Suddenly the bright headlights of the machine stabbed out into the snow-packed yard. Mike started down the road heading for the creek with his mother following close behind lighting the way with her tractor's lights. Mike finally left the plowed roadway and began wading through thigh deep snow toward the creek. He moved upstream about thirty yards to where the creek made a sharp bend. He paused to overlook the terrain. He knew that Skipper used to sit here a lot watching the waters flow swiftly past. He didn't say anything to his mom; he just pointed and then stepped aside.

Libby jockeyed the tractor into position through the deep snow, dropped her bucket and the stabilizers for support, swung around in her seat, and began to dig. Breaking through the ice-covered ground was difficult. The tractor bucked and danced as Libby forced the case-hardened steel teeth of her backhoe through the frozen earth. Finally a big slab of icy dirt was pried free and placed aside. Libby dug now in soft earth beneath the snow. Several scoops were sufficient.

Libby climbed from the seat and pulled a spade from its bracket on the boom. She dropped into the deep snow and stepped down into the shallow trench. She worked with the spade smoothing out the ground, hollowing out the soft dirt for Skipper's final resting place. Her breath drifted in sporadic clouds about her face as she labored and the blue white smoke of her tractor's exhaust floated lazily across the swift moving creek. Mike all this time stood quietly by holding his friend for the last time.

Libby motioned for Mike to come. He moved forward, stepped down into the hole with his mom. Together they placed the little dog into the grave. Mike took the spade and carefully began covering the bright blanket. Libby swung back up into her seat on the tractor. At last it was done. Mike stepped clear and Libby used the backhoe to push the dirt back into the hole. Finally she lifted the solid block of frozen earth and placed it atop the small mound. In the spring the grave would receive its final landscaping.

Mike climbed to the frame of the tractor as Libby drove back to the shelter of the barn. Neither of them said anything during the quiet evening hours.

Mike was off to school the following morning, apparently none the worse for his watery experience the day before. Libby had been silently, and with great apprehension, watching the calendar through all of these trying days. She was focusing on January the nineteenth, the date of Bill's death. She couldn't get the date out of her mind. Yet suddenly here it was. She had said nothing to Mike about it, hoping that the moment would slide by unrealized. Hopefully it would spare him from reliving another unpleasant and regrettable memory. Today was the dreaded anniversary that she had tried so hard to put aside. She was planning to take Mike to town tonight for a special prime rib dinner at the local restaurant. This he always enjoyed. Hopefully an evening of extracurricular activities would also shield her from some of the grief that she felt building.

Libby found that the day was far from being normal. The routine happenings around the resort went almost unnoticed. The hands of the kitchen clock ticked slowly toward the mid afternoon moment when the sheriff's deputy had knocked on her door exactly a year ago. What was her name? Oh yes, Deborah... Yes, Deborah Newman. Libby remembered the moment all too well. At 2:25, she pulled on her outside garments and walked out the front door into a light snowfall. She uncovered her log splitter by the woodshed and spent over an hour splitting and stacking a good-sized pile of firewood. She pushed herself relentlessly even to the point of stopping for a moment to remove her cumbersome heavy coat. She still wore her fleece-lined leather vest, finding it sufficient as long as she kept working and didn't slow down. With grim determination she placed the final chunks neatly on the top of the stack. She was pleased with herself. Although remembering all too well, she had not broken. She had just relived the experience, word for word, moment by moment. Libby had not shed a tear; she had remained in complete control.

After school Mike delivered a supply of wood to one of the cabins with a wood stove and replenished the supply at the main house. While he was doing this Libby showered and slipped into a fresh pair of jeans and a good shirt. Mike met her in the kitchen a few minutes later.

"What's for supper, Mom?" he asked.

"Whatever you want to order. We're going out on the town tonight."

Without comment Mike headed for the bathroom and washed up enough to be presentable. While he was doing this Libby informed her guests that she was going out, but would be back soon. She gave each of them her cell phone number just in case.

It was a pleasant and uneventful evening. At no point did Mike mention his dad's passing. They were back at the resort well before bedtime. Libby spent nearly an hour with her computer and phone catching up on a reservation request that had come in during the evening. Libby stepped into Mike's bedroom and glanced over his shoulder. He sat at his desk sketching another clipper ship in the course of weathering a black and angry storm. She shook her head sadly, and a frown rippled across her forehead. Mike had not forgotten, he remembered all too well. This she sensed even though there was utter silence in the old family home.

CHAPTER XIII
Resolution
January 20–March 15, 2000

The rest of the winter went well. The weather began to moderate. The creek rose every day as the deep snow began to melt. In the valleys rain showers added to the flood. Libby finally stored the snowmobiles in the old barn for the season, and uncoupled her snowplow from the front of her pickup. The air was progressively warmer with each passing day. February was gone and March was bringing the first of the spring wildflowers. The mountain air had a damp, wet, fragrant, sweetness about it, as the deep snowbanks melted away exposing the frozen earth to the sun for the first time in over four months.

One Saturday about the middle of March they returned to Skipper's grave. Mike had spent several days after school preparing the small plot of ground beside the creek and outlining the area with smooth rocks from the creek bed. It was, for the most part, a silent service. Mike had carved a simple nameplate with only the name "Skipper." He forced its stake into the hard ground at the head of the small grave.

Mike rose and turned back toward the house. "Bye, Skipper," he said. "I'll always remember you." It was a solemn hour following the service, but by midmorning things had returned to normal.

That week, Libby invested a modest sum in the purchase of six mountain bikes, which she offered to her guests free of charge. Mike and Brenda enjoyed these versatile modes of transportation, spending occasional evenings back on the old Forest Service trails. They took off on the bikes one evening leaving their parents resting on the front porch of the house.

Gordon and Libby had both had busy days, in their own ways, and were quietly enjoying the solitude and their cans of beer.

Libby suddenly broke the silence. "Can I borrow two horses for a day or so?"

"Sure. I'll bring them up any time you say. Have you got a place to keep them?"

"Yes. Mike and I fixed up that old corral behind the barn a couple of weeks ago. They can get under cover too, and there's a watering trough there as well. I'm going to fence off a few acres up on the hill later on. When I get that done, I guess we'll buy ourselves a couple of horses; then I won't have to beg and borrow all the time."

Gordon threw an arm about Libby's shoulders and gave her a big hug. "You can borrow from me anytime you want, Libby. When do you want them?"

If you could drop them off on either a Friday or Saturday evening that would be fine. I want to take Mike back into the hills for a quick tour. We won't stay overnight or anything like that."

"Want me to come along? Brenda would like the ride too."

Libby hesitated, slightly embarrassed. "No, Gordon. Not this time. I'd like this trip to be a private, family time."

"OK. I understand. I'll drop them off on Saturday sometime. I'll bring the makings for supper that night and the kids can ride during the afternoon. You'll have them all to yourselves on Sunday. You can keep them longer if you'd like."

"That sounds great," Libby remarked. "But I won't need them after Sunday evening. Thanks anyway."

Libby was cleaning up two cabins on Saturday morning when Gordon pulled into the main yard. Mike ran from the woodshed, where he had been splitting firewood, to greet their company. Libby watched from the cabin windows as she worked. The horses were unloaded and led back to the corral. Saddles and other items of the riding gear were carried into the barn. Gordon backed his stock trailer up to a secure place beside the shed and uncoupled it from his truck. He and Mike unloaded three big bales of hay from the pickup and stacked them beside the corral.

Much to Libby's surprise, Brenda came down the hill to the cabins and stayed with her while she finished her cabin cleaning. They were done quickly and, lugging big armfuls of dirty linen, they walked up the hill to the house together.

The two families had a great day. The kids rode for several hours in the afternoon and curried and groomed the two mounts when they were done. A new client arrived in mid afternoon, but after that it was peaceful and quiet in the valley. Gordon fired up the propane barbecue and did justice to the huge steaks that he had brought for their supper. Libby threw together the remainder of their meal. They all sat on the porch after dark watching spellbound as a full Montana moon struggled to push itself above the rolling hills off to the east. A tall stately pine silhouetted against the lunar disk struggled to keep the moon in place, but failed. As the moon broke free, Gordon and Brenda headed for home. Libby and Mike turned in a short time after their friends departed.

It was midmorning the following day before Libby's chores were done and they were ready to ride. Mike was a big, strong boy. Yet, Libby was surprised when she found the two horses already saddled and eager to pull out. Mike was taking after his dad as far as his height was concerned, still Libby had no idea that he could handle the heavy riding gear. He had somehow managed to get the bridles on the animal's heads too. It was obvious that he had watched Gordon carefully, and he had learned well.

When Libby arrived from the house she had a large package wrapped in a blanket that she tied securely behind her saddle. Mike used the lower rail of the corral as a cheater step and climbed aboard his mount. Libby swung quickly and easily aboard hers.

"What's in the bundle?" Mike asked.

"A snack for later," was the simple reply.

They rode for a ways along the Forest Service road. Where snowmobiles had packed the deep snows down hard, there were still patches of white, and back under the towering trees they found some snow that hadn't melted as yet. Libby finally left the main Forest Service road and turned off on a seldom-used trail.

She twisted around in the saddle and called back to Mike. "I used to ride up here quite often when I was a kid," she explained.

They climbed higher and higher along the narrow switchback trail. In open areas the warm sunshine of spring had done away with the winter's accumulation of snow, but in the sheltered sections there was still plenty. Twice they encountered the upper reaches of the east fork of Gomas Creek. Both times the creek was found thundering down vertical rock cliffs fed by melting snow, year-round springs in the high country, and Iron Fork Lake. The stream was too dangerous to ford, but Libby didn't seem to want to be across the waterway in any case.

She finally left the faint trail and angled off through the timber. There was a solid blanket of snow almost everywhere at these elevations. They rode for perhaps an hour and then suddenly Libby cut sharply to the west and began climbing steeply. With a surge she stretched out along her mount's sweaty neck and broke from the heavy cover at the edge of the forest. Her horse's hooves rang crisp and clear on the open bedrock of the mountain only recently free of its carpet of snow. Libby followed a long upward slope of barren granite for about a quarter of a mile. They were climbing steeply along the shoulder of the mountain, and ahead there was only blue sky where the granite pathway seemed to come to an end. Libby finally pulled her winded mount to a halt. The big sky of Montana loomed before them.

"Wow!" Mike muttered as his gaze swept the open country before them.

Libby swung down from her mount. "Thought you'd like the view," she replied.

A brisk westerly wind whistled across the rocky knoll carrying with it the fragrance of warm sunshine on barren rock. The smell of damp muddy forest floor on either side of the ridge, and the crisp scent of melting snow and ice from far above made their contribution to the majestic scene. On the horizon rose tier after tier of snowcapped mountains stretching upward toward the Idaho border. In the distance they could see several clearly defined areas where logging had taken place and the second growth timber was growing dense and green once more. Far below could be seen the rolling foothills, and if you looked closely enough, you could pick out several tiny clusters of buildings. But near at hand there was little sign of man's encroachment on the virgin landscape.

Mike dismounted. Libby pulled a pair of hobbles from her saddlebag and attached them to the front feet of Mike's horse. Her mount, according to Gordon, was well broken to being ground reigned. Still Libby was cautious. She tied the ends of her reigns to the front legs of her horse just below his fetlock joint. He wouldn't go running off now.

Libby hung her Stetson from the horn of her saddle. "I used to come up here every now and then when I was a kid," she said. "I'd just sit and watch the world go by, ever so slowly. This is a wonderful place to think about yesterday, about today, and about tomorrow."

"Sometimes I don't want to think about yesterday," Mike replied solemnly.

Libby nodded. "I know what you mean."

Mike walked ahead and stared down into the nearly endless expanse of timbered valleys. "Dad would have liked this place."

"You're right... I told him all about it many times." Libby walked up beside her son. "Yes, he would really have loved the view." She placed her arm about Mike's shoulders and they stood thus for several long silent moments nearly spellbound by the grandeur spread out before them.

At last they walked back to their horses and from the saddlebag Libby withdrew a folded burlap sack. She loosened the cinch of her saddle and began rubbing down the hot sweaty mount. The animal, you could tell, enjoyed the rough burlap against his hide. Mike followed his mother's lead. Libby gave each mount a small amount of water in the crown of her battered Stetson. They drank with enthusiasm before she returned her canteen to the saddle.

Libby put her hat back on; and from behind her saddle, she retrieved the blanket-wrapped package containing their lunch. She unfolded the wool covering and spread out their small feast. The polished mahogany box with the brass bindings was set unceremoniously aside. Mike grabbed a piece of cold fried chicken and a warm can of Coke and settled down on the blanket beside his mom. There were carrots, celery, sliced ham, and bread to supplement the fried chicken. They ate heartily while their gaze wandered about the vastness of their mountain world. A ground squirrel darted up over the edge of the ridge and with a zigzag course hesitantly approached the picnickers. Mike threw him a small piece of bread crust, which he immediately crammed into the pouch in his cheek.

They were soon done eating. Libby began to pack up the remnants of their meal. She at long last reached over and picked up the brass bound box, which had thus far been deliberately ignored. She held it in both hands in her lap for a long minute.

"You know what this is, Mike?" she asked quietly.

There was a long pause as Mike gathered his thoughts. "That's Dad's ashes," he finally replied.

Libby just nodded. She fumbled with the latch on the box and finally opened the lid and withdrew the small ceramic urn. She set the box aside and slowly rose to her feet.

"When they presented me with this, I wondered what I would do with it. Most people remember some sensational place that was really meaningful to the departed person. I couldn't think of anywhere that was really appropriate. Then I remembered my childhood trips up here. Your Dad loved to hear me talk about this place, and he always wanted to come here someday and see for himself... One year we almost came when he had his vacation. I wish now that we had... maybe if he had seen... if we had moved here, he wouldn't have..." Libby slapped her thigh sharply with her open hand. "Enough!" she almost shouted. "Enough," she muttered again.

It was silent for a long time with only the sigh of the wind and the occasional sound of a horse nervously rattling his bit, or stomping an impatient hoof. A stellar jay landed on the shattered limb of a bristlecone pine that was struggling to survive at the edge of the granite outcropping. He challenged the group, blending his raucous voice to the whispered chorus of sound. The ground squirrel edged closer, and Mike tossed him another tidbit for his midday snack.

"You going to spread Dad's ashes on the rocks here?" Mike asked quietly as he stared down at his feet and kicked absently at the smooth bare surface of the mountain.

"I'd like to just give his remains to the wind and let them rest wherever seems best." It was quiet again for a long minute. "Of course, Mike, if you object or have another idea I'd love to hear it."

Mike shrugged. "He was your husband, Mom."

"Mike? He was your father!"

"I know. I'm not objecting, it's just a little hard to come right out with a decision."

"You want to think on it for a while?"

"No, Mom. It's OK. I think Dad would like his ashes to be in this wild untamed world."

Libby nodded. They didn't speak for several minutes. Then she opened the small container, turned sideways to the gusty wind, and began to gently shake the ashes from the urn. The gentle breeze whisked the remains away in a thin gray cloud. She stopped and passed the container to Mike. He hesitated a moment and then fed the remaining particles to the wind. Only a few tiny bits dropped to the rocks by their feet. The majority of the ash was carried far away to fall on the timbered slopes below. It suddenly seemed very quiet on the mountain. Not a word was spoken. Mike turned, capped the empty urn, and returned it to the ornate storage box.

Libby wrapped everything in the blanket, tied it securely to her saddle; and they were soon ready to ride. They swung into their saddles. Mike had a tough time but managed. His upper body strength carried the day. Almost as an afterthought, they abruptly reigned about, just for a moment, for one last look, one final memory.

"Good-bye, Bill. I love you…" Libby whispered. "God be with you." She reigned her horse away, back toward the timber. Mike turned toward the hidden trail in silence.

Sometime later as they dropped from the granite ridge into the trees, Mike pulled up beside his mother. "That was what they call closure, right?"

"I believe so," Libby replied. "I think I feel a little better all ready. Maybe I'm not so much of a widow anymore. Of course we will each have our memories, but it's important now for us both to focus on the future."

"I think you're right, Mom. It will be fun over the years to ride back up here. I'll know that Dad's out there somewhere in the mountains making things grow, making the world a better place."

Libby didn't reply, but unseen tears flooded her eyes. Mike dropped back slightly, as they wound their way down the narrow trail heading for home. It was almost dark when they finally reined in by the corral.

"I'll rub the horses down and feed them," Mike suggested. "You can go and fix supper."

"Why? You hungry?" Libby asked with a big smile suddenly replacing the somber expression that she had carried for the past few hours.

"Better believe it."

CHAPTER XIV
The Long Hot Summer
March 16–July 1, 2000

The following morning, Mike rubbed down and fed Gordon's horses before he headed off to school. He seemed to really enjoy working with the animals. For Libby it was a routine day. Two guests checked out leaving two units to be cleaned up and readied for the next occupants. Libby went back into the hills in the afternoon and cut up one small dead and down tree. She had just begun unloading the small load from her truck when Mike came up the road from school. He stopped and helped unload and then vanished into the old shed where he began working on his tractor. Gordon came by after work driving his big Dodge pickup. He and Libby hooked up the horse trailer and loaded the equipment and animals.

Libby raised the ramp and closed and locked the back door of the trailer. "Want a cool one?" she asked.

"That sounds like a winner to me," Gordon replied.

They walked together to the house. Gordon stopped on the porch and seated himself on the top step while Libby continued on into the house. She returned a minute later with two cans of beer and an open bag of pretzels. They sat side by side in the shade provided by the over-hang of the porch roof.

Gordon motioned to the cabins on the slope below them. "You full up?" he asked.

"No. Three empties over at the lodge and two cabins. The three lodge spaces are due in sometime today. They're part of a Chicago church group's outing. Leased the whole lodge for two weeks. The empty cabins are booked again starting tomorrow."

"Full house then."

"Except that tomorrow the other three cabins go empty. Lots of housework tomorrow afternoon."

Gordon chuckled. "And you love every single minute of it."

Libby laughed. "Keeps me busy and out of trouble. I'm going to hire a local woman to help with the housework now and then."

"Hey! I'm all for that. You and Mike work too hard sometimes."

Libby laughed. "That will free me up for some other chores like repairing that old barn, irrigating, cutting fire wood, and going to town."

They talked and sipped their cool beers for several minutes, but then a Chevy Suburban pulled into the drive and proceeded slowly up to the house.

"Looks like you've got company," Gordon muttered. "Guess I'll take my critters and head for home. Give Mike my regards, and thank him for taking good care of the horses. They looked great."

Libby placed her empty beer can on the step and walked down to greet her arriving guests. Gordon crossed over to his truck and trailer and a moment later drove carefully down the steep grade from the house to the Forest Service road. He vanished into the timber a moment later. Libby checked her guests in and went with them to the lodge where they were greeted by their friends from Chicago that had arrived earlier.

The next day Libby bought a pickup load of fencing supplies including steel T posts, hardware, a post driver, and barbed wire. On the hill behind the main house she paced off and marked what was probably five acres of fairly good ground. One side of this area terminated at the old corral that she and Mike had already repaired. The area was situated just inside of the main irrigation line so they could keep the area well watered during the summer months. When Mike came in from school that day Libby showed him the truckload of fencing supplies and introduced him to the post driver.

"Oh boy! We're going to get our own horses," he exclaimed.

"Maybe someday, but we've got to have a fenced-in field before we can get any. It's going to take awhile too," Libby explained. "This will only be a temporary fence. Someday I'd like to put in good cedar posts and wood rails instead of barbed wire."

They began their project that very same evening by running a long string from the corner of the barn to the upper corner of the proposed enclosure. It was right at one hundred yards. They sprayed a chalk powder spot every eight feet along the line to mark the position of each post. They followed just outside of the irrigation line across the backside.

In several places trees came down across the line. They would use these as fence posts wherever possible. The long backside of their field would be about six hundred fifty feet in length. It was past suppertime and almost dark before they came back to the barn and corral with the last leg of their fence line.

"I'm going to start supper, Mike. You go back around and count the number of blue dots that we painted. Let's see if I've bought enough posts."

A half hour later Mike came into the kitchen. "How many posts did you buy?" he asked. "And what's for supper?"

"Spaghetti. The ticket's on my desk. I think I bought two hundred."

Mike went to the office and returned a moment later. "You're right, Mom. Better go get thirty-seven more."

"Go figure out how long it will take us, if it takes thirty minutes to drive each post."

Mike reentered the office and returned a moment later with a pocket calculator. He leaned against the counter beside the stove and began punching buttons. "Glory, that's a hundred eighteen hours." He stabbed the pad several more times. "Darn, Mom. If I work just three hours after school every day it'll take me thirty-nine days to drive all those posts."

"Don't forget, you have the weekends too." Libby was smiling to herself as she stirred the sauce for their supper. "You could also take a lantern out there and get a few more done before bedtime."

Mike frowned. "I know you're pulling my leg, but it's still going to take forever. And we have to put up all the wire too."

"That's right. Four strands of barbed and one of electric."

"Oh, wow. I won't get the field ready until next summer," Mike complained, emphasizing the word next.

"Don't forget you have a mother," Libby chuckled. "I'll help. It'll be a big job, but I think we can get it done way before fall. Remember school's going to be out in June, and the days are getting longer too." Libby pretended to count on her fingers. "You could get probably thirty-five posts a day once school's out."

"You really think I can do that many?"

Libby laughed out loud. "If you did you'd drop dead. That's tough work driving those posts. I drove a few when I was a kid. It's really hard work. Sometimes there are rocks in the way that you have to work around. It takes time and lots of effort. But don't worry. Together we'll make it, and hopefully by fall we'll have a good horse pasture where Gordon can keep his horses if he'd like to. I just don't want you to think that this is any small project. Come on. Throw some plates on the table. Let's eat."

From then on driving fence posts seemed to be their only form of recreation. The heavily weighted post-driver was essentially nothing but a four-foot length of heavy steel pipe about six inches in diameter. It had handles welded on either side of its open lower end, and the upper segment was solid iron. In all, it probably weighed at least twenty pounds. The top of a steel fence post would be placed within the driver with the lower end of the post positioned where the post was to be driven. When it was stood upright and its vertical alignment verified the driver would be pushed upward and then slammed down with all of a person's strength. This driving motion would continue until the post had been driven as deep into the ground as was desired. Sometimes the post drove easily, other times it was quite the opposite.

No longer did Libby have spare time moments to sit on her front porch, sip a cool beer, and watch the world go by. Most days Libby used her leisure time well. She managed to drive a few posts in the hard ground. Mike contributed several more each day along with his other chores and his homework. They were making good time. It became obvious that they would have their fence completed by the end of April.

This hard manual labor was toughening the hands of both of the fence builders. At the beginning of the project, they had the misguided conception that their hands were already toughened by plenty of hard work; but the post driver was proving them wrong. Their heavy gloves didn't seem to be doing them much good either. They had blisters on top of the blisters, and several times they called a halt to their undertaking for a needed day of rest.

Arm and shoulder muscles were taking a beating, but Libby realized that all of this hard labor was beneficial. Ever since her return to Montana, there had been a noticeable change almost on a weekly basis. All of the sessions at the fitness center back in Pennsylvania had kept her body attuned for the real exercises of everyday Montana life.

She began to feel great, better than she had in many years. She felt, with tongue in cheek, like she could arm-wrestle almost anyone and walk away the champion.

Libby was watching closely too as Mike grew in stature. He had always taken after his dad in the height category and was already just over five feet tall. He was suddenly gaining weight every day with not an ounce of fat anywhere on his young body. It was all muscle, sinew, and bone.

By mid-April the posts were all in place and they stored the post-driver, hopefully forever, in the tool room in the barn. The wire came next. It was always a two-person job. First the heavy spool of wire had to be unrolled along the ground. After that one person would use the stretcher to pull it tight, while the other fastened the strand to the steel posts.

The barbed strands seemed to have minds of their own, snaking, twisting, kinking, and snagging anything they could get their barbs into. No matter how careful the fence builders were, the barbed strands attacked them time and again. The wire had the tenacity and savage personality of a she mountain lion with kittens. Libby bought a jumbo-sized package of Band-Aids to keep pace with their numerous cuts. Their old work clothes were becoming tattered and torn and were ready for the ragbag by the time the barbed strands were all in place. The standoff insulators and the bare strand of electric fence wire were the uppermost items to be attached to their enclosure's sturdy posts.

It was the springtime holiday called May Day when Libby turned on the power to her completed fence. The charger clicked rhythmically and everything worked just fine. Libby picked up a long blade of Timothy grass and placed it on the electrified wire where her fingers were about ten inches from the wire. Very slowly she pushed the blade of grass across the strand. Her fingers were about six inches from the wire when she stopped.

"Yeah, I can feel it. Here, Mike. You try it." Libby offered the blade of grass to Mike, but gave no words of warning or caution.

Mike took the grass and placed it on the wire. He immediately shoved it across the electrified strand. Suddenly he let out a yelp of pain and surprise; shaking his hand vigorously, he threw the grass wildly away from him. He had gone too quickly, closed the gap too much, and had received a good jolt of harmless electricity for his troubles.

Libby apologized. "Sorry, Mike. I just couldn't resist. It's all controlled voltage. It gives you or the animals a good jolt, but it really won't hurt you." Mike was not overly impressed by his mother's apology and explanation.

They irrigated their new upper field and the areas around the resort about once a week keeping everything lush and green. About twice a month Mike mowed the resort grounds giving them a well-cared-for look. Libby often buzzed around the foundations of all the buildings with a weed-eater tidying up the landscape.

The weather was unseasonably warm, almost hot, as day after day the southerly winds blew dry parched air across the mountains. Normally the westerlies carried a higher degree of humidity and brought occasional rain showers to the valleys. But the unusual southerly wind, and almost drought conditions plaguing them this year, brought no rain. Be that as it may, their small creek still rattled down the valley, fed by its alpine lake, several springs, and constantly melting snow in the higher elevations.

Gordon and Libby sat on the porch in lawn chairs one evening. Mike was busy changing a set of sprinkler pipes stretching across the open land below the house, while Brenda teased him continuously from the sidelines. Mike dropped the final section of pipe into place and the line burst into action with the numerous sprinkler heads clicking rhythmically as the spurts of water blasted out across the terrain. Mike was heedless of the cold spray. He stopped a sprinkler head in its rotation and aimed it directly at Brenda. She thought she was outside of the range of the sprinkler, but she was wrong. The two kids began chasing one another in and out of the pulsing streams of water. In less than a minute they were drenched running back and forth, in and out, of the refreshing spray.

"Want to go see if we can catch them?" Gordon asked half rising from his chair and reaching for Libby's hand.

She jerked her hand quickly away. "Not on your life," she almost shouted.

The kids ran down across the road, reached the bank of the swiftly running creek, and just jumped in.

Libby laughed. "I hope Brenda can swim," she remarked.

"I hope so too," Gordon replied half rising from his chair.

Libby reached a restraining hand out to Gordon's arm. "Don't worry, Gordon. It's not that deep. She can stand if she needs to. Mike's a good swimmer, but I wonder how long they'll be able to stand that darn cold water." Libby just shook her head.

The current swept the two kids quickly downstream. Brenda was paddling hard, managing to stay afloat. Mike meanwhile had rolled onto his back and was just letting the current carry him. The tide deposited them on a gravel bar just below the cabins. They crawled out and, having had enough of the cold water, headed up the hill toward the house. By the time they reached the porch they were passably dry.

Libby's new cleaning woman was working out well. This freed Libby and Mike for some other duties, or just a short period of leisure time. In June school was out; and Gordon, Libby, and Mike went to several horse sales. To Mike's chagrin they didn't find just what they were looking for. They reluctantly decided to wait until the big fall sales in October when ranchers were thinning their remudas prior to the onset of winter.

The resort was doing well, and Libby and Mike spent many days back in the hills replenishing the wood supply. Gordon was absent from the scene for two weeks in late June. He and his horses were involved in a joint two-county search-and-rescue mission over in Silver Bow County. Libby hated to admit how much she missed his company when he was away.

On the first of July Libby left Mike at the resort and went to town to do some long overdue shopping. The town of Boder appeared as it normally would on a heavily overcast day. But today it wasn't cloud cover that blotted out the sun; it was a low-lying smoke haze drifting through the canyons. Many small forest fires were burning, but so far, none threatened the small settlement.

Libby left town heading home, and just outside of the city limits sign, a large mule deer and her fawn leaped from the side of the road right in front of her. Libby slammed on her brakes and swerved quickly for the shoulder. There was no sickening thud. They were all lucky. The two deer made it across the highway unharmed, and Libby ended up on the gravel shoulder of the road with no damage at all.

Libby glanced up in her rear view mirror. Luckily there had been no one behind her. She heaved a big sigh of relief and just sat there watching the two animals as they wandered peacefully out across the fields on the far side of the pavement.

At last she started to turn once more onto the road. As she glanced back she caught a sharp reflection of red and blue lights from the vicinity of a house sitting far back from the roadway. A single ray of sunlight broke through the haze and fell on a county police cruiser sitting beside the small log home. The beam of light had caught the warning lights on the cruiser's roof perfectly. Parked under a tree was a big Dodge 4 × 4 and next to the small barn a large tandem axle horse trailer. It was too much of a coincidence to be ignored. Libby knew about where Gordon lived just outside of town, but in all the confusion of their hectic lives, she had never actually visited his home.

Instead of going on, she made a quick U-turn in the highway and backtracked about a hundred yards to the appropriate driveway. The mailbox carried only a box number. She drove slowly to the house and parked beside the cruiser. As she climbed from her truck she saw movement in the corral behind the small barn and walked in that direction. She found Gordon rubbing down one of his horses. Libby stopped by the rails, folded her arms comfortably across the uppermost timber, rested her chin on her arms, and waited for him to notice her. A long minute passed, and then he moved to go around to the other side of the horse. He jumped noticeably as he spotted his visitor.

"Well I'll be damned," he muttered. "How long you been standing there?"

"Awhile... I like to watch you work. When did you get back?"

"This morning, 'bout ten I guess. I called the house and talked to Mike."

"I missed you, Gordon."

"I missed you too. Come on let's go in the house. It's a little cooler in there."

Gordon slipped through the small gate in the corral and joined Libby as they headed across the lot toward the house. He reached out and slipped his arm about her shoulders, and with a little skip Libby adjusted her stride to match his. Libby circled his waist with her arm and hugged him closely. They entered the house and Gordon immediately swung around and took Libby full in his arms and gave her a big kiss.

An old German shepherd rose sleepily from his bed in the corner, came close with an air of caution, and nosed Libby's hand warily for several moments. About his neck was a heavy leather collar. Libby caught a glimpse of a silver and gold badge as the dog turned away. With a sigh he returned to his bed, flopped down, and went fast asleep.

"That's Sergeant Jethro," Gordon announced. "Poor old guy is just a shadow of what he used to be. He can't understand why his body has betrayed him. He's over fourteen years old now... Used to be a great police dog. I was his handler for ten years. He's retired now... Want a cold drink, Libby?" he asked.

"Love one." Libby glanced around at the typical man's home. It was neat and orderly, but could use a woman's touch, that was for sure. She dropped down on the floor beside Sergeant Jethro and began stroking his massive head. The dog took a very long deep breath, opened his eyes for a moment, and then with a sigh went back to sleep.

Gordon came back into the room; and Libby rose, crossed to the heavy leather couch, and settled herself comfortably on the cool soft surface. Gordon joined her a moment later.

"I really missed you a lot," he said as he slipped his arm about her shoulders.

It was quiet for some time. Libby sipped at her 7-Up, enjoying its cool freshness. She found that she was also enjoying Gordon's touch as he stroked her shoulders, upper arms, and the long soft strands of her ponytail. She tossed her battered Stetson aside, and finally turned to face him kissing him eagerly several times. There was a moment of indecision on both of their parts, but then they kissed for real, hard and passionately.

"Oh God, Gordon, I missed you so much."

"Dance with me," he suggested as he rose from the couch.

He extended his hand to her. She cautiously rose and discreetly slipped into his arms. He kissed her again and began exploring the richness of her body as they swung to an inaudible tune. Libby suddenly found herself gasping for breath, teetering on the invisible barrier that had always existed between them. She glanced around and saw what appeared to be the doorway leading to Gordon's bedroom. She held him close and with determined steps maneuvered him slowly toward the dimly lit area. They slipped into the small room, and Libby reached back with her foot and kicked the door closed.

CHAPTER XV
Red Skies
July 1–August 30, 2000

Gordon walked Libby out to her truck some time later. She slipped into her seat, rolled down the window, and tossed her old Stetson over onto the seat beside her. Libby turned and folded her arms across the window ledge. She looked closely at Gordon for a long silent moment and then reached down with her right hand and started her engine.

"Thank you, Gordon... Supper about six?"

Gordon shook his head. "Sorry, Libby. I've got to work tonight."

"I'll give you a rain check. Come by when you can." Libby leaned out her window and Gordon bent forward and kissed her one more time. She was gone a moment later.

Libby reached the Gomas Creek turnoff from the main highway and pulled to the side of the road. She sat for several minutes looking southward up the valley carved by the north fork of the Clamis River. The smoke haze was heavy drifting down the valley, and in the distance she could see an actual smoke cloud billowing into the hazy skies. She had heard of the Rosen Gulch fire and knew they were having a bad time over there. The rest of the way home, she thought about her own fire plans, just in case. The stark reality was, she had no plans. She pulled into the resort complex and found Mike with a garden hose washing the front windows of the house. The small hose and the billowing smoke clouds she had seen up the valley just didn't seem to be compatible.

"Hi, Mom," Mike called. "Gordon called awhile ago. He's back."

"I know. I saw him in town."

Libby sat down on the steps of the house and let her eyes roam across the resort, its buildings, the timbered slopes, and open areas surrounding them. Mike finished his window washing and came over to sit beside his mother.

"There's something on your answering machine," Mike said.

"I'll check it later… When we irrigate all this grass between here and the cabins, we've got enough pipe to go the full length of the cabin row, don't we?"

Mike didn't hesitate. "Sure, plenty of pipe left over. Why?"

Libby leaned back and hooked her elbows onto the floor of the porch. "Just thinking."

"About what?" Mike asked leaning back like his mom.

"Fire."

Mike shook his head. "That fire's a long way off, Mom. It won't ever get this far," he exclaimed.

"But what about a different fire? One that started right down by the main road?"

Mike thought for a while. "The fire department in Boder would come and fight it, wouldn't they?"

"They don't have to. We're not inside their jurisdiction… The Forest Service has a couple of pumpers. They could help, but right now they're tied up with bigger blazes. Sometimes they just let the fires burn out on their own.

"You know, Mike? It's an uphill slope from the cabins to here. They're not very tall buildings. If we set up a line of irrigation sprinklers along the hill above the cabins, and tipped the sprinkler heads away from the buildings, I'll bet the streams would squirt high enough, and far enough, to keep the roofs well watered down."

"How we going to make them tip the way we want them to? Mike asked.

"A stake in the ground and some bailer twine tied to the top of the sprinkler pipe. We could tip it just as far as we wanted."

"What about the lodge and our house? And the barn?"

"All we can do is wet everything down real good with a hose and hope for the best."

"Yeah, and hope the fire truck gets here," Mike replied.

Libby laughed. "Well, in the past few days we've irrigated about everything we can reach. It's fairly green and damp all around the buildings and in the new fenced-in pasture, but we should aim our sprinklers back into the timber again as far as we can. Let's wet the whole darned canyon down at least a little."

"You're worried about the fires, Mom," Mike said. His voice pointed to a reality, not a questionable condition.

"Oh... I don't know. A little maybe. Let's see... I've been thinking... Those sprinkler heads shoot a stream about forty feet. We might as well get ready. Take the pipe trailer and run a line along the slope about fifteen feet up hill above the buildings. I'll go get a bunch of stakes and some bailer twine. I'll tell the guests what we're doing so they can close the windows in the cabins for a few minutes while we try it out."

Mike loaded a bunch of pipe on the trailer and drove along the slope installing the sections. Libby drove stakes and tied each riser pipe to the stake pulling it over at an angle. Curious guests watched and a couple of the men pitched in and helped out. At last they were ready to test the system. Libby turned on the valve from the main line and the sprinklers began their rhythmic click, click, click. For the most part the arc of the sprinklers was too far and Libby started down the long line adjusting the tie-down strings to the proper length. An hour later all was complete and the line was shut down. By this time Libby was drenched, head to foot, and she retired to the house for a dry change of clothes. It now appeared that they could put up a wall of water to protect all of their cabins from airborne sparks and embers carried by the wind from any fire in their area. Whether it would be enough protection had yet to be seen.

The following day Libby went to Missoula and purchased a large, heavy duty, portable fire pump. It was gas engine driven and had a long heavy suction line that could be placed into a creek or pond. She bought five hundred feet of one-and-a-half-inch fire hose, the maximum length recommended for her pump's capacity, and an adjustable nozzle. Their fire pump came mounted on a trailer and could be towed behind their pickup. They tried it out when they got it home. Mike threw the suction line into the creek while Libby connected one length of fire hose to the pump. She started the engine and Mike grabbed the nozzle.

"Turn it on, Mom," he yelled.

Libby opened the valve. The canvas hose swelled and stiffened as the water surged through the hose. It reached the nozzle and a moment later Mike let out a scream as the powerful stream of water bursting from the nozzle knocked him from his feet and sent him sprawling across the grass. He finally managed to gain control, but could only physically sit on the hose, pinning the powerful nozzle to the ground with both hands. It would be a two-person job to control this monster. However, it was obvious that the stream of water thrown by the pump and its hose was enough to keep the main house and barn well watered down. Reaching the entire lodge building would be a problem. Prepared as they were, Libby had seen similar endeavors in past years go awry. Property owners, although battling furiously, had to retreat before the onslaught of fire, losing everything.

Almost every night Gordon called. His days were very busy with traffic control, road closures, eviction notices, and just plain routine happenings. He and Libby discussed her fire precautions, and Gordon continued to voice an optimistic viewpoint concerning the resort's location.

The Rosen Gulch fire had spread to double its size, and in the neighborhood of twelve new blazes had sprung up across the upper reaches of the valley. The Big Sky of Montana was rarely seen. At night, dry lightning storms crashed about the mountains, many times starting new blazes. The wind blew almost constantly from the south bringing nothing but very dry air. The ultra-low humidity, and soaring daytime temperatures, were fanning the blazes. Pilot Dome erupted in towering flames after a dry lightning strike on the first of August. This blaze was only two miles southwest of them and sent rolling smoke clouds scudding before the wind. They could easily smell the acrid odor of burning forests. At night there was a dim red glow in the western skies as the light from surging towers of flame reflected off the ever-present smoke haze.

"Is it coming our way, Mom?" Mike asked with a note of concern edging his voice.

Libby stretched her legs out onto the hard ground by the steps where she sat. "It's getting close." She pulled her big red handkerchief from her hip pocket and mopped the sweaty surface of her face and neck. "They're using Gomas Creek and the main road for a firebreak. I saw two retardant planes from Missoula making runs along there this morning. Listen close, Mike. Every now and then you can hear helicopters back in that direction. If the wind changes we'll start wetting down the house and lodge. But right now we're doing all right."

"The lodge is empty now, Mom. Where did they all go?"

Libby laughed. "I gave them a refund and they got the hell out while the getting was good. Just one couple left in one of the cabins."

"And us," Mike replied. "Somebody's coming," he announced, gesturing toward the road.

The forest service pickup, its strobe lights flashing brightly, rolled up to the house and Ted Lewis climbed out. He, like his truck, was covered with dirt, ashes, and mud. He hadn't slept, shaved, or washed in days, it appeared.

"Hi, Libby… Mike," he greeted. The ranger leaned back against the cab of his truck.

"What can I get you, Ted?" Libby asked.

"Water, and lots of it," Ted answered with a tired grin. He reached into his truck and tossed an empty canteen to Libby. She in turn passed it to Mike. The ranger unslung an empty canvas water bag from his side mounted rearview mirror and tossed it to Mike.

"Pretty bad out there?" Libby asked.

"Getting worse. The damned wind is starting to swirl around. Can't tell where it's blowing from."

Mike returned and handed the full canteen to the ranger and placed a tall glass of ice tea from the refrigerator into his dirty hand. Mike hung the full water bag in place on the truck's mirror.

"Oh boy, thanks. This is great… Look Libby, I've been watching your preparations out here. I admire you to no end, but it's time to get the hell out of here. I don't think Gomas Creek and the highway are going to stop this monster. Look at it." He turned and gestured with his arm toward the far ridge. "We've closed Gomas Creek Road ten miles north of you to all traffic coming this way."

The ranger pointed to the steep slope just west of them. It was on the far side of the creek and the roadway. The trees at the top of the ridge were silhouetted against a backdrop of billowing clouds of smoke. The smoke in several places had a red-streaked tint to it as flames licked at the mountain just beyond their field of vision. A large twin-engine tanker plane from Missoula suddenly burst from the smoke cloud streaming the final drops of its retardant chemicals along the face of the ridge. It banked steeply and headed north, passing almost directly overhead.

Libby swallowed hard. "It's not coming our way, Ted. Look at the smoke."

The ranger nodded. "Right now it's not, but you're too damned close, Libby."

"I'm not running. We've got everything ready and we're going to fight it."

"Here comes Gordon, I think," cut in Mike.

They turned and watched the county cruiser, with all its lights flashing, as it swept up the hill toward the house. Gordon climbed out and shook Ted's hand.

Ted pointed to Libby. "Gordon, you talk some sense into this stubborn damned woman, will you?"

"She won't leave, I take it," the deputy replied.

"She can't stay here. The wind shifts even a little and she's had it. Look, down there it's crossed the crest of the ridge already."

"Libby? Gordon began. "Take your guests and you and Mike get the hell out of here. Ted's right. This could change for the worse at any time."

"The road's still open?" Libby asked.

"Yes," both men replied in unison.

"It's open down to the main highway," Gordon added.

"Then I can retreat if I have to. Right now I'm not giving up. If worse comes to worse, I'll go sit in the creek till it passes."

"At least let me take Mike out with me," Gordon pleaded. I'm going to advise your guests to get out too. How many are there?"

"Just one couple in cabin number three."

Mike spoke up. "I'm not going, Gordon. It takes two of us to hold that fire hose."

There was a long moment of silence finally broken by a helicopter as it thundered along the face of the ridge. The two officers stood and looked at each other shaking their heads.

"Thanks for coming by, guys. Better go and check on other folks. We'll be all right here. If worse comes to worse, Gordon, I'll meet you at your place down on the highway when it's over."

The two officers shrugged. Gordon stepped up to Libby and gave her a big kiss, much to Mike's surprise. The ranger frowned for a moment, and then tried hard to suppress a smile. Then the two officers climbed into their vehicles and left Libby and Mike by the porch. Gordon stopped by the cabin and warned the occupants there to get out, and then he too vanished down the smoky road. The guests were not far behind.

Libby placed a five-gallon can of gas beside her fire pump and covered it with a heavy canvas. The long fire hose was connected and stretched out to a position between the barn and the main house. A weak point to Libby's plan was that she couldn't reach the back side of any of the big main buildings. The water from her big hose could soak the roofs, the front, and the ends of the house and barn that was all. Mike had two small garden hoses connected behind the house and barn and another on the backside of the lodge. Maybe these would help. Irrigation sprinklers were clicking away in several places along the edges of the timber, but the line protecting the cabins had not been turned on as yet. The tense hours dragged slowly by.

Mike went to the house. Libby sat in the front seat of her pickup parked beside the porch and watched the billowing, sweeping, towers of smoke above the ridge. Three deer trotted up the Forest Service road, paused to drink from the creek, and then moved farther east into the tall timber.

"Here, Mom," Mike greeted.

Libby turned to look at her son. He was holding a peanut butter sandwich out to her with his free hand. In the other hand he held an open can of Coke.

Libby took the sandwich. "Thanks. You see the deer a couple of minutes ago?"

"Yeah. Think they know something that we don't?" Mike asked.

Libby laughed for a moment. "Maybe they're just a little more cautious."

Libby and Mike moved one of their sprinkler lines to a different area, which seemed to be a little dryer than some other places. Darkness was finally trying to settle in above the haze of smoke when Gordon pulled into the yard driving his own pickup.

"What are you doing here?" Libby asked.

"Taking a vacation… You know something? I have twenty-six days of compensatory time built up, not counting two weeks of sick leave.

They thought it was a rather inopportune time for me to suddenly want to be off, but I did some explaining and they sent me on my way."

"That explaining must have been something."

"Oh, it was, but I had to invite them to our wedding as well."

Libby swung about quickly. "Our what?" she blurted.

Mike rose from the steps. "Whose getting married?" he asked, suddenly very alert.

"I hope your mother will marry me," Gordon answered.

Mike frowned. "I suppose that will make Brenda my sister."

"I don't know about that, but we'd be one family anyway."

"We've got a good big field for your horses, Gordon."

"Yes, I know, and we..."

"Hold on, you two. Don't I have any say in this?" Libby cut in.

Before anyone could answer a retardant bomber from Missoula thundered directly over the resort, banked hard, and discharged a long plume of bright orange chemicals along the face of the ridge.

The people remaining at the resort realized that it was nearly dark now, and most of the light was being reflected from the fire. The raging flames threw their brilliance back from the low layers of smoky clouds swirling about the small valley. Suddenly there was an explosion and the skies above the ridge blossomed in bright tongues of flame. The whole northwestern horizon, as far as they could see, was suddenly involved. The trees around them, the buildings, even the ground seemed to tremble, such was the force of the blast.

"It just crowned," Gordon yelled. "Look at that devil!"

Libby pulled her big bandanna from her hip pocket and tied it across her face. She pulled on her heavy work gloves. With a very quiet, level, controlled voice, she turned to Mike. "Go start the pump, Mike, and turn on the sprinklers for the cabins when you go by. After that, you watch the back of the house and barn. Do what you can with the little hoses. Keep an eye on me and Gordon. Remember, the creek's our last resort. You be careful, and take your key from us. If we run, you follow. Don't try and be a hero."

Mike nodded his understanding and dashed off to start the fire pump. Gordon and Libby walked over to where the fire nozzle lay on the wet grass. As they watched, a twinkling shower of embers began to fall all about them. Suddenly the sprinkler line began to pulse and the cabins were blanketed by a torrent of water. A moment later the roar of their big fire pump filled the air, the fire hose at their feet suddenly became as hard as iron.

A Forest Service truck pulled into the resort, its amber caution lights flashing, and about a dozen black-faced firefighters climbed out. They split up in two-person teams and moved off into the timber both east and west of the resort. They carried axes, shovels, and chain saws, and several of the men had Indian pumps strapped to their backs.

Gordon picked up the nozzle, braced his feet, and pulled the control handle back. The pump roared as the governor kicked in. Libby grabbed the hose just behind him absorbing part of the kickback, and together they began a sweeping motion pouring water on the roofs of the house and barn. Over their shoulders they could see the blanketing effect that Libby's stationery sprinklers were having on the row of cabins. Sheets of mist from the sprinklers and clouds of spray from the hose nozzle swirled about them. They were soon both drenched.

Burning embers and tiny glowing sparks fell in swirling clouds. Most extinguished themselves almost immediately when they come to rest on the damp ground. Now and then one would land on bare skin and would be quickly swatted away. Gordon had a smoking, charred spot on the shoulder of his shirt that had gone unnoticed, and Libby reached up and slapped the hot ash away.

"Let's hear that again, Gordon," Libby began, shouting to be heard above the noise.

Gordon glanced back quickly at Libby. "What?" he shouted.

"You know, what you were saying about a wedding," Libby hollered back.

"Oh, that? Hell, Libby, Mike's all for it. He thought it was a good idea."

"Aren't you even going to give me time to think about it? Hey, swing over to the back end of the barn."

Gordon braced his feet and swung the hose where directed. Just then a Green Forest Service fire truck pulled up into the resort with its red warning lights flashing. Three rangers, or maybe just firefighters, were aboard. They assessed the situation quickly and moved closer to the lodge. They began running a line over to the lodge. In minutes the roof of the building was soaked. Libby and Gordon's line was able to cover the main house and barn complex quite well. A Forest Service semi-tanker truck arrived hauling a full load of water for the pumper truck. For nearly three hours they battled the rain of falling embers from the huge blaze. Then suddenly, almost as quickly as it had begun, the wind shifted, and the sparks stopped falling. Gordon shut off the nozzle and the roar of the big pump dropped to an idling whisper. Mike appeared from behind the house dragging a small garden hose. Libby walked down and closed the big valve, shutting down the sprinkler set aimed at the cabins.

Very slowly silence and darkness seemed to slide into the valley. There was only a faint glow from above the ridge across the creek. In twos and threes the firefighters that had dispersed into the timber to catch spot fires traipsed back into the resort. There were about twenty people gathered about the fire truck. Ted Lewis arrived with his amber caution lights flashing. He climbed from his truck and looked about, checking for damage. Everyone was black with smoke and ash. Libby ran to the house and a minute later returned almost dragging a laundry basket about half full of beer and cold drinks. There was a cheer among the men as they all gathered round.

"We stopped that bloody, damned, son of a bitch, that time," one of the men yelled as he popped the top on a can of beer.

"Watch your language, Carl. There's women and children present," someone shouted.

The bearded firefighter bellowed back. "Shit, Andy, them two can walk beside us men anytime."

"Hell the lady's systems stopped it, we didn't," someone yelled.

"Guys, that fire crowned across the top of the ridge, one of the rangers explained. That's probably all that saved any of us. It blew itself out."

There were many muttered agreements and disagreements concerning the demise of the main front of the fire. Libby turned to Gordon, caught his arm, and tried to lead him away from the group. "I still want to know what you and Mike were talking about when you mentioned a wedding?"

"Who the hell's getting married?" one of the smoke-blackened fire-fighters asked having overheard the question.

"I am," Gordon called back over his shoulder.

"To who?" someone else wanted to know.

There was an uncomfortable silence for nearly a minute as every eye in the group was focused on Libby, awaiting her answer.

Mike finally broke the uncomfortable silence. "To my mom, that's who," he shouted back.

"Oh my God," muttered Ted Lewis. "A conspiracy."

Libby began to laugh, and then she began to cry. Gordon took her in his arms and held her close. One of the rangers picked up the nozzle of the fire hose, aimed it straight up into the smoke-riddled sky, and opened the valve. The icy cold water of the creek poured down over everyone in the group and Libby began to laugh again. Mike joined his mom and the deputy, and as the first light of dawn began to struggle into the smoke-filled valley, they headed for the house.

— 0 —